perfect partners

Stephanie Cage

CRIMSON
ROMANCE
F+W Media, Inc.

Published by
Crimson Romance
an imprint of F+W Media, Inc.
10151 Carver Road, Suite 200
Blue Ash, Ohio 45242

www.crimsonromance.com

ISBN 10: 1-4405-6341-1
ISBN 13: 978-1-4405-6341-6
eISBN 10: 1-4405-6342-X
eISBN 13: 978-1-4405-6342-3

Dedication

For Steve, my perfect partner,
with thanks for everything.

Chapter 1

"So what's he doing back in London after all this time?" Lisa asked, leaning in the doorway of Elaine's office, dangling her silver sandals by their straps.

"Don't do that to your shoes," Elaine said. Lisa automatically set her shoes down beside her on the rough carpet. She envied her dancing coach's commanding tone—no wonder Elaine could keep mobs of unruly eight-year-olds in check better than anyone. "He came back because he heard about Jerry's accident and knew you'd be without a partner for Blackpool."

"Yeah, he says." Lisa turned her eyes to the row of trophies on the top shelf of Elaine's bookcase, then back to her dancing coach, who was smothering a smile. "That's got to be up there on the list of great lies of all time. Number one—looks don't matter, it's what's inside that counts. Number two—size doesn't matter, it's what you do with it that counts. And number three—I did it all for you." This time the smile didn't stay smothered. She waited for Elaine to stop chuckling before she continued. "I bet he says that to all the women on the cruise ships."

"He says? Lisa, when did you last read the news?"

"Never. I'm a marketing exec, not a news reader, in case you hadn't noticed."

"Cheeky." Elaine gave her a sideways look, and Lisa wondered if she'd gone too far. Among the studio's part-time teachers, she was known as the sweet one who didn't snap or answer back. But then, she didn't normally have to deal with the prospect of facing, for the first time, the guy who'd broken her heart when she was eighteen. No, make that the guy who had taken her heart and smashed it into tiny pieces and trampled them under the suede soles of his dance shoes.

It had taken her two years to get over him enough to get together with someone else, and even that hadn't been a resounding success. She couldn't have married Brandon, not even for her mother's dying wish. What had she been thinking of? And for five years, no less!

For that matter, what was she thinking of now, drifting off into a daydream mid-conversation?

She tuned back in, just in time to catch the last of Elaine's comment. "...and ended up with a studio in Florida."

Oh. So that was all she'd missed. A news flash on dancing's golden boy. No longer roaming the world chasing rich widows and a perfect tan. Now that he was working in the States he had it all in one place, while she struggled to fit her real passions, dancing and teaching dance, in the gaps around a demanding day job in marketing. Well, good for him. It didn't change anything as far as she was concerned.

"Oh," Lisa said faintly, trying not to think of Redmond eight years older, wiser, and probably sexier. With a tan.

"So..." Elaine quirked an eyebrow. Lisa had known her long enough not to have to ask what she meant. Would she or wouldn't she? And how Lisa wished she could say no. No, I won't have the bastard back under this roof with me at any price. No, I won't dance with him at Blackpool. And no, I absolutely will not under any circumstances let anyone believe for a moment that there's anything going on between us. I don't care if the TV crew thinks that following half a dozen couples who are real-life partners as well as dancing partners would make great TV, or if they are putting up an eye-popping sum of money for the best couple at the end of the series. It's not worth it, for the trophies or the money, or anything else.

But...

Even though Elaine tried to keep the pleading out of her voice, Lisa knew how much it would mean to her and Mark. They'd been almost like parents to her for years now. She owed them. Winning at Blackpool would be a big deal for her career and for the studio. The money would help too. If they got the big prize, it would take care of all the repairs the cinema-turned-studio needed, and stop the directors getting in trouble with the listings committee over using cheapskate suppliers. Even if she and Red didn't win, well... six weeks of prime time TV... Lisa knew money couldn't buy that kind of advertising. Certainly not the kind of money that a beautiful but antiquated studio rapidly being overtaken by shinier, newer venues could afford. She loved the Empire. She didn't want to see it close...

If only she could have danced with Jerry. OK, it would be a hard push to convince the TV producers, who wanted to film real-life couples who danced together, that her lanky gay friend was her partner in life as well as on the dance floor, but they'd escorted each other to weddings and family occasions once or twice in the year since she split with Brandon and at least she'd always had a laugh. It had been so easy.

As easy, whispered a treacherous voice in the back of her mind, as things had once been with Redmond, before he disappeared off to the ends of the earth, with not even a postcard to show for it after that first summer.

She didn't want to remember, but how could she forget? She could imagine him here now, lacing his dance shoes and stretching out his long, lean legs as he waited to hear her verdict as to whether she'd take part in the show... not that it had ever been in any doubt.

Her mouth opened itself before she was conscious of having made a decision. With a final mental curse for Jerry going and injuring himself just two months before the big day, she told Elaine, with not a trace of the terror she felt, "OK, I'll do it."

Elaine whooped.

"If he really wants to," Lisa added. "And if we still dance OK together."

It was her last let-out.

"Well, you don't need to worry about the first. He was the one who suggested it. He's waiting downstairs, so he can join us for practice tonight. And you'll be good together. You always were."

"Hmm."

That was what Lisa was afraid of.

She picked her sandals up more carefully under Elaine's watchful gaze, and marched down the stairs, head held high. No way was she going to let anyone see that his return made any difference to her.

Maybe it wouldn't. Maybe when she saw him again she'd realise that he was, after all, just a man like any other. Maybe then the spell would be broken and she'd be free to settle back to real life again, without the dream nagging at the back of her mind as it had been for the last eight years.

Maybe. She didn't believe it for a moment. She still remembered the first time he'd appeared at the studio, and the almost physical reaction she'd felt. It wasn't the first time she'd seen him. They'd been at the same school for ages but in different years. He was a macho football fanatic, while she concentrated on her books and her dancing, so they'd never had much to do with each other. Then she'd walked into the dance studio one wet spring evening, a little early for her class, and found herself pausing in the doorway, her eyes drawn to one young man who looked somehow familiar, though for the moment she couldn't place him.

He was a little taller than the other boys in the class, dancing the same steps as everyone else but with twice the energy and a smile so bright that the dingy room felt a million times lighter. It was only when a grapevine brought him almost face to face with her that she placed him as the guy she'd admired from afar for so long. She hadn't expected to find him dancing, but now that he was, it was no surprise to find him doing it stunningly.

Even after the best part of a year as his dancing partner, she'd still been awed by his energy and excitement. A little of it had seemed to rub off on her, too, so that she smiled a little more widely, spun a little more swiftly, and stepped a little more gracefully than she would otherwise have done.

She wondered, as she stepped off the last stair and prepared herself to face Redmond again, whether the magic would still be there. Then she wondered whether she hoped it would, or feared it.

"You can do it," Lisa told herself. As she reached for the door of the main practice room, she took a deep breath to steady herself, as she did before stepping out onto the floor for a competition. She was, after all, a performer. Dancing competitively was as much about acting as it was about footwork. She'd pulled off bigger acts than this before.

She straightened her back and flung the door open.

He was leaning against the wall, as tall and lean and languid as she remembered. His dark hair was cropped a little more closely, making him look younger than she'd imagined him, and his skin was nearer to coffee-coloured than it had been when he'd left London.

"Oh, hi," she said, knowing that she sounded lame and kicking herself for not thinking of a witty opening remark. She forced herself to tear her gaze away and sat down on a bench to buckle on her Latin sandals.

"Hi, yourself. You sound surprised. Didn't Elaine warn you?"

What kind of warning was ever going to prepare me for this? she wanted to ask.

"She said you were here." Lisa didn't add that, in her recollection, "he's waiting for you downstairs" could mean anything from "he got here twenty minutes early and stormed off in a huff ten minutes ago" to "he rang ten minutes ago to say he was leaving." Elaine had always had the good sense not to get in the middle of their quarrels. Smart woman.

Redmond straightened and held out a hand to her. "Shall we dance?"

No apology, no pleasantries. Just straight to work. Well, what had she expected? Roses and a red carpet? The most romantic thing he'd ever bought her was a fish and chip supper. Though, come to think of it, eating fish and chips under the stars with him on the promenade outside the Winter Gardens at Bournemouth had been one of those perfectly peaceful moments that had sometimes come back to her with a stab of regret as she'd squabbled with Brandon across a restaurant table someplace in Kensington. Well, you couldn't have everything, could you? She needed a dance partner, and she wasn't going to get better than Redmond Carrington, Junior British Open and twice Ten-Dance Champion.

What was he doing here? Outside the floor-to-ceiling windows, traffic queued nose-to-tail up to the traffic lights at the end of the road. A driver honked repeatedly as the Shepherds Bush bus pulled out from the bus stop into his path. On the common, one hardy dogwalker watched his black Labrador chase a crisp packet across the thin, muddy grass. And Redmond had left a comfortable job in Florida for this and the promise of a medal and five minutes of fame? It didn't stack up.

But she couldn't think about it forever. He was standing over her, waiting with infinite confidence and patience for her to join him on the dance floor.

Lisa never turned down an opportunity to dance.

She stood up, dropped her fleece onto the bench, and took his hand, willing herself not to notice the way his strong fingers encircled hers, making her feel safe and protected. Whatever his body told her, it was a lie, she told herself. He'd never been anything but trouble, and he never would be. Their partnership was a convenience, nothing more. But his hand on her back, where her low-cut dress gave way to bare flesh, still felt warm and firm and right. And when he shifted his hold, her body still responded, sending soft shivers down her spine.

He pressed the play button on the CD player as he passed, and after a moment's pause the music began. Even though they were dancing a rapid jive, skipping and spinning and dipping, she still had time to notice how his eyes were fixed on her with almost frightening intensity. That was something she'd forgotten about him. The way he did everything as if his life, or maybe more than that—the fate of the world—depended on it. It was as if time stretched when they were dancing. In between heartbeats he could move his feet in perfect unison with hers, adjust his routine to avoid other couples on the floor and fit around her occasional slips, and still favour her with a long, lazy smile whenever she followed a particularly tricky move.

Finally, just as Lisa was becoming breathless the track began to slow down. Redmond's effervescent energy softened to an easy swing, and as the music drifted to a halt, he swung her into a slow, languorous drop.

Lisa had never liked drops. She never quite trusted the men who threw her from one hand to the other like a juggling ball or swung her like a limp rag. Spinning, she had always felt in control, but when she was caught and lowered rapidly until her hair brushed the floor, it made her nervous. She did it anyway, of course, because she was a professional, and she never complained. But every time she was lowered to the floor, her knees felt weak and her head whirled with images of the hard tiles flying up to meet her: the crack of bone, the metallic smell of blood, the pain.

Of course, she'd known Redmond would do it sooner or later. Men always did. They liked to show they were in control. Difficult moves are a boast—more to the other men on the dance floor than to the woman in their arms. I can make her do anything I want, they say.

And he could. He always had been able to. She stopped thinking as he drew her closer, spun her around, twisting his arms under and over hers. She didn't need to think, because her body followed his effortlessly, as it always had. When he pulled her into his arms and leaned her gently towards the floor, she felt like a child being laid down to sleep. It was like coming home.

For a long moment she basked in the feeling, and then the music picked up again—one of those terrible cheating false endings, making her think it was all over when it was just the beginning of a new phase of the medley. Redmond must have known it was coming, because as the pace picked up again, he was right with it, flipping her upright and into a spin and a rapid flick-step, which she had to work hard to follow.

He must have seen this, because next time they came face to face, he used the opportunity to look searchingly into her eyes and ask, "Still OK?"

"Fine." She grinned, wishing she had the breath left for a longer, more positive answer. But the important thing was not to have given in. She wouldn't be beaten—by the dance, by Redmond's irrepressible energy, by anything. Anyway, it was true in a sense, she excused herself. She was dancing, and she was following the steps. If they danced like this in the competition, they'd do well. That was all he was asking, all he cared about. He didn't want to know about her wobbly legs or her pounding heart or the taut feeling in her throat. He didn't care about her. It was just dancing.

Only it wasn't just dancing. It never had been. Maybe with Jerry and some of the others it had been something close to "just" dancing. There wasn't intimacy there, or the wordless communication so perfect that sometimes she thought she was dancing steps before they were led. Somehow she knew that this time, when the music slowed to a real ending, he'd draw her in close to a sway and a lean, and hold her for a long moment as she gazed up into the sky-blue of his eyes…

When he released her, she was unprepared for the briskness of his response.

"Good. The drop wants some work. You're still fighting it a bit, but I think we'll get there. How's your waltz?"

Well, two could play at that game.

"Pretty good," she said, knowing that he knew she wouldn't have said as much if it had been anything short of perfect. "How's yours?"

An unnecessary question. Nothing Redmond ever did was far short of perfect, but if she hadn't asked, he'd have known she remembered. She didn't want to do him that courtesy. He didn't deserve it.

"Want to find out?" He held his hand out, confident of her response, as if no woman had ever refused him a dance. They probably hadn't. Competent male dancers were rare enough; competent, good-looking, and considerate ones still rarer. And he was, she reluctantly conceded to herself, all of those things. Well, mostly considerate, she amended, remembering his abrupt disappearance all those years ago, and the dismissive way he'd summed up their first dance today. As if it was all her fault and she wouldn't fight him if she trusted him. Well, she'd have trusted him if he'd been more trustworthy. So it wasn't her fault.

Why did he always put her on the defensive? She shook her head and followed him to the corner of the room as the intro to the waltz ended. Right on time, he swept her into his arms and slipped into a smooth, graceful stride.

She'd almost forgotten dancing could be like this. Her feet kept time with the music all by themselves, and she felt as light as thistledown floating in the wind. Now that it was dark, the windows reflected, and overlaid on the London night she could watch the ghostly image of a stunning couple drifting in perfect synchronisation along one side of the floor. In her heeled dance shoes, she came just above his shoulder, and her long brown hair tumbled in waves down to where his strong hand rested on her back, guiding her. The couple hung in a hover just long enough to allow her to admire the effect, and then took off again, weaving and spinning their way into the centre of the floor. It was a variant of a waltz routine they'd put together for a show shortly before Redmond left. You couldn't have danced it in a competition—too much risk of collision as it took a sweeping path right through everyone else's routines. Not that Redmond cared much what other people were doing. He'd dance around them when he could, and through them when he had to. But this was too much even for him. So it was nice to dance it again, on a wide-open floor with nobody else around to dodge.

Lisa was conscious that her eyes were getting that dreamy expression they did when everything came together perfectly. It didn't happen often. She could count the number of times it had happened since Redmond left on the fingers of one hand. Hell, on one finger. It didn't happen dancing any more. She'd been starting to wonder if it ever had, or if it had been a daydream cooked up by her adolescent mind. The only feeling to compare was when one of her friends had brought her new baby home from the hospital, and Lisa looked down at the tiny, peaceful sleeping face and thought that the world seemed like a wonderful place to be.

She didn't know if Redmond could see the smile creeping across her lips, and she didn't want to find out. She snapped her lips back to the expressionless line she'd chosen to adopt with him, and set about making conversation.

"You seem to remember all our routines pretty well."

It had sounded innocuous enough when she'd thought of it, but now she regretted admitting she'd recognised the steps as the ones they used to dance together.

Redmond's lips curled in a smile that was broader and cheekier than she remembered.

"You remember the routines? Maybe I'm making it too easy for you," he suggested, in a mock-innocent voice she remembered only too well. "Let's see what we can do about that."

And then he spun off into a series of pivots that left her even more breathless, followed by some complicated footwork that she'd never danced before and suspected she'd never recognise if he were to dance it again. That, in turn, swept into a kind of sway. She leaned into it gracefully, but without the first idea what he was trying to achieve.

"Raise your left leg and lean in. That's it. A bit further. Good, but don't let your topline go."

She strained to keep her head in the correct position, feeling awkward and off balance. She hated being told what to do, but couldn't fight it because she suspected that, if she didn't feel so awkward, the new step would be a great addition to their routine. Damn the man for always being so... well... right!

Because of course he'd even timed the sway perfectly so that as he swept her up and out into a dizzying spin, the music ended.

She knew she ought to be pleased that after all these years her perfect partner was back when she needed him most, but it galled her to realise how much he'd moved on. He'd learned so much, while she'd plodded through medals classes and workshops and danced the old familiar routines with partners who were never quite as good as Redmond had been.

She wanted to be furious with him, but she didn't have the luxury. She needed him too much.

"Not bad." He nodded. Lisa could see him assessing their performance, working out what needed to be done to bring it up to scratch for competition. Not too much, she thought—they were pretty nearly as good as they'd ever been, but then the opposition at Blackpool was pretty good too. Fritz and Kathrin especially, but David and Caroline were solid performers too. She and Red would be battling it out as part of the top three, she thought. Well, a top three place would be great, but if she knew Red he wouldn't settle for anything less than first.

"Another dance?" This time she got in first.

Red checked the clock above the door and a frown flitted across his face. "Sorry, I've got to go. I've got a call to make. Same time tomorrow?"

A call? Big deal. How important a call could you have to make at eight in the evening? And if he really had to make it, couldn't he do it here, in the café or a spare practice room, and then get back to practice? But no, as always, everything of his came first, and she had to fit into the gaps. Damn him.

"Sure," she murmured through gritted teeth.

Chapter 2

When five-thirty came around, Lisa was sitting in a client meeting, fuming. She was supposed to be at the studio in half an hour, which would be possible—if she left now. But the client, Gary, had been talking for an hour and showed no signs of stopping. Even more annoyingly, so far he'd come up with nothing that couldn't have been handled in a one-page email. Just more and more suggestions for improving the three mailshot mock-ups she'd given him. He was supposed to be choosing one, but it didn't look as if it was happening. She'd given up being discreet about looking at her watch, but he still didn't seem to notice. She deliberated slipping out to call Elaine and ask her to tell Redmond she was running late, but that would only delay things further, and surely Gary would get to the end soon.

Or not.

At quarter to six he was still rambling on, and they were no nearer a conclusion. Desperate measures were called for.

"I tell you what," she said, in her best brisk, hurrying things along voice, "why don't I take your suggestions on board and send over the revised versions tomorrow, and then you can let me know which you prefer?"

He looked as if she'd snatched the rug from under his feet, but after a moment he capitulated.

"Shall we have a call at two-thirty?" She had meetings from three till five, and she'd need the morning to make all the changes. Now she'd landed herself with three times as much work, but at least she was out of the office for the time being.

She showed him down to reception and breathed a sigh of relief. If she was quick, she'd only be a few minutes late to the studio, and it wasn't as if Redmond had never been late himself. In fact, she half expected to rush in panting and find the studio still empty. It wouldn't be the first time. Still, that didn't stop her fidgeting fretfully as she stood at the bus stop.

Ten to six ticked by, then five to.

Two buses came past, but didn't stop.

She rummaged in her bag for her mobile and failed to find it. For a moment she thought she'd lost it, but then a vivid image flashed into her mind of her desk as she hurried past to show Gary out. A flash of silver peeked from under a pile of papers. The phone. She hadn't even checked for messages to make sure the practice session was still on.

Finally, when she'd more or less given up hope and decided to go and find a payphone, the bus turned up. Two minutes to six.

It was six exactly when Lisa fell into a seat as the bus pulled out into the heavy traffic of West London in rush hour.

She pulled out a book and tried to read, but the words swam in front of her eyes. In her mind, her feet were dancing through their old routine, and a thousand Lisas and Redmonds swept and spun their way gracefully around a mirrored hall. They looked so right together. But then, who was she kidding? He was so stunning, he'd make anyone look good. It didn't mean anything... except that she had a better chance of winning at Blackpool, and maybe even the TV competition, with him than anyone else.

Maybe that was enough.

She almost believed it, until she hurried into the studio shortly after quarter past six and the door banged shut behind her with an empty echo. Then the lurch she felt in her stomach betrayed her. His absence was like a blow. She'd lost him once already, if you could call it losing him when she'd never had the nerve to do more than hint at her feelings for him. It had always been impossible to tell whether his casually flirtatious manner towards her hid a deeper attraction, or was just the habit of an attractive man far too used to having women fall over themselves when he snapped his fingers. Maybe there had never been anything to lose, but it had felt like a loss just the same when he left, and Lisa couldn't bear to let herself start hoping again.

"Looking for Redmond?" Elaine asked from the doorway. Her voice was casual, for which Lisa was grateful, but there was a trace of sympathy in her eyes.

Lisa steeled herself for whatever was to come.

"Has he been here?" she asked, willing her voice not to sound desperate.

Elaine nodded, her eyes wide and expressive. Once again Lisa wondered how much Elaine knew, or guessed. Elaine had never asked, but now and again there was a hint in her manner: the diffidence when she suggested Redmond as a partner, the sympathy when, yet again, Lisa arrived to an empty practise room. Lisa had so hoped that he'd have developed some consideration over the years, but apparently that was too much to expect.

"Did I miss him by much?" She forced her voice to stay level, to betray neither annoyance nor desire. She wasn't sure it had worked, but if Elaine saw anything she knew better than to acknowledge it.

"Ten minutes."

So he'd left only minutes after the time they'd agreed to meet.

She thought back bitterly to the times he'd kept her kicking her heels on an empty dance floor for half an hour or more.

"Nice of him to wait."

Elaine gave a wry smile. Lisa could see she was thinking, as everyone always had, that Redmond was a law unto himself. He arrived or he didn't. He stayed or he didn't. Never according to any rule that anyone else could figure out—in fact, as soon as you thought you'd worked out what he was going to do, he'd do the opposite, even if you'd already taken into account the fact that he'd do the opposite of what you expected.

"He said he had to make a phone call. Get some dinner and he'll meet you in the café at half past."

Lisa nodded. It could have been worse. He hadn't actually abandoned her for the evening. He was coming back. Still, it set her teeth on edge the way he assumed she'd be at his beck and call, sitting there waiting for him when he chose to join in. For a moment she was childishly tempted to plead a phone call of her own, or a forgotten prior engagement, and rush off into the night, leaving him to sit and wonder.

What prevented her was not an absence of spite, but an excess. There was no point in trying to wind him up, because it never succeeded. There was always a queue of pretty girls waiting for him to beckon them onto the dance floor. If she vanished, he'd probably never even notice.

Lisa bowed to the inevitable and picked up her handbag.

"Shall I bring you back a coffee?" she asked.

"No, I'm fine, thanks. Anyway, I don't drink coffee," Elaine said, smiling. She often teased Lisa about the way she used "coffee" to refer to hot drinks in general, even though neither of them drank it.

Lisa switched her dance sandals for outdoor shoes and walked round the corner to the small café where the dancers tended to congregate between classes.

She leaned on the shiny chrome counter and pondered the menu. She normally ate after practice, but then she'd normally had a decent lunch. Thanks to Gary's volubility, she'd only managed to grab half an egg mayo sandwich for lunch, and now she was ravenous. She ordered soup and a roll, and sat down to wait.

As she waited, the door opened and Jerry came in, wobbling slightly on crutches. She waved him over and he sat down, propping the crutches in the corner of the booth.

"How's the walking wounded?" she teased. She didn't make a habit of joking about injuries, but with the grin on his face she guessed it was safe enough.

"Wounded," he answered, pulling a long face but with a twinkle in his eye.

Lisa smiled. Jerry was so effortlessly likeable. At that moment she'd have given anything to have him back as her partner for the championships. Rehearsing with Jerry had been so easy and lighthearted. He was as different from the prickly, complicated Redmond as a kitten was from a porcupine. Why, oh why, did he have to get injured?

"Guess what?" he added in a loud stage whisper.

"What? Oh no, wait, let me guess. You've met the love of your life?"

"How did you know?" Jerry pulled a wide-eyed astonished face, and Lisa laughed. This happened routinely at least once a month.

"Haven't you always?"

"This is different. I really think he's the one."

Lisa shook her head. He always did, right up until the moment they stood him up, took him for a ride, or ran off with one of his younger, cooler colleagues. But it never seemed to sour him. He laughed, shook himself off, and moved onto the next.

Sometimes Lisa wished she was more like him. Easy come, easy go. Life would be simpler that way.

Instead, here she was stuck with an aching longing for the most infuriating man she'd ever had the misfortune to come across.

"What about you?" Jerry asked as he always did. "It's time you were settling down and thinking about little Lisas." Jerry loved kids more than anything and, as he was always pointing out, the chances of having any of his own were vanishingly slim. "I want my godchildren," he demanded petulantly.

"Oh no." Lisa rolled her eyes. "Here we go again. Anyone would think you were my mother." Not that she'd had to put up with that for the last few years. Her mother had died of cancer, still believing that Brandon was going to take care of Lisa for the rest of her life. Since then, Lisa hadn't been allowed to forget about parental pressure, though. Her friends were always saying how their mothers were pushing for grandchildren. Most of them were in steady relationships with nice guys and if she'd been in their position Lisa might have been thinking about kids, but they all seemed to be more interested in their careers. Lisa's career bored her silly. Dancing was another matter. That would be hard to give up, but then it wouldn't be long before her kids were in the toddlers' class themselves...

She rolled her eyes. For a moment, she'd let Jerry get to her. It wasn't going to happen.

Jerry was watching her closely. She took a deep slurp of soup to hide her embarrassment, only to embarrass herself further by choking on the hot liquid. She coughed and gagged into her serviette. Suddenly strong hands were on her shoulders and an amused voice from close behind her drawled, "What have you been doing to her?"

Jerry gave a stagy shrug. "Wasn't me, guv."

Lisa took a hasty sip of water and turned to find herself staring straight into Redmond's chest. His right hand still hovered protectively over her shoulder and he was gazing down at her with an unreadable expression.

She felt herself blushing. The only thing worse than making such a fool of herself in front of him was the thought of what she might have said if she hadn't choked.

"Of course I want kids," she'd been thinking. "I just want them with the right man." What an invitation that would sound! Not that it would occur to him to take it that way. After all the glamorous women on the cruise ships and the young American girls with their siliconed beauty, he would never look twice at Lisa except as a dancing partner.

She looked at the floor and waited for her cheeks to cool. Redmond was chatting amiably away to Jerry, with not a word about her lateness or his disappearance.

Jerry had on his trademark rueful smile and was waving a crutch, so she guessed they were talking about his accident. It didn't look as if she was going to hear more about the latest love of his life today, but no doubt he'd be back tomorrow to tell her more, if it hadn't all worn off by then.

The waitress came over with Jerry's coffee, and he hauled himself to his feet and turned away. Redmond slid into the empty seat beside her.

"Bye," she called to Jerry's retreating back, annoyed at his abandonment even though she knew he could have no idea how much she hated to be left alone with Redmond. That was the worst thing about this crazy competition set-up. Now she had to act delighted at his presence even as she squirmed inside.

"You OK?" he asked, still smirking a little. "I didn't mean to startle you."

Great. Now he thought it was his doing.

"Nothing to do with you," she said brightly. "Just something Jerry said."

Not that she was going to give him the satisfaction of knowing what.

"You've made your phone call?" She knew she sounded a little sharp, but she couldn't quite resist reminding him how he'd left her waiting. Again.

"Mmm hmm. I hope you didn't mind. When you were late, I thought you'd probably come straight from the office and wouldn't have had time to eat, so I suggested to Elaine that you come round and get some tea. Don't want you turning faint on me while we're practising."

"So considerate," she murmured. It was irritating to know that it only mattered to him because she wouldn't be such a good dancing partner, but at least he'd thought about it. That was, a nagging little voice told her, more than most men would have done. Jerry, for all his kindness, never troubled his head with concerns about what she did when she wasn't dancing with him. At least until it came to the matter of godchildren…

Her thoughts were wandering again. She dragged them back to the present.

Redmond was talking, but she'd missed the beginning of the sentence and she wasn't about to admit to disappearing into a daydream. She tuned back in and tried to pick up the thread of the conversation.

"…everything's OK. I wanted to ring early, rather than after practice. Some conversations you need to be at your best for."

He was excusing the phone call, she assumed. A girl back home? She should have guessed. What was Redmond doing back here after all this time anyway? Family business, Elaine had said evasively, and oddly. Redmond didn't have family here any more. His father had passed away two years ago. Redmond had flown in for the funeral, and out again the next day. Lisa hadn't even found out he'd been home until Elaine had let it slip a fortnight later.

Now Redmond was back on the subject of dancing. Safe. She tuned back in with a guilty start.

"Shall we give the tango a run-through?" he asked.

Tango wasn't until a later round of the show. If they didn't make it past the waltz and jive, they wouldn't need to dance it. She supposed that suggested confidence, which was gratifying.

She agreed and got to her feet. Redmond turned away, stuffing a piece of paper into his pocket. She was fairly sure it was handwritten, and bore a stamp. Who on earth wrote letters nowadays? She'd have asked, but that would have suggested altogether too much interest in something other than the dancing.

As she followed Redmond out of the café, she found that her smile was beginning to creep back. She couldn't quite suppress her excitement as she stepped through the studio door and sat down to pull on her dance shoes. That done, she grabbed the first CD that came to hand and popped it into the player.

It was a relief to be back on the dance floor. Even though it meant she could no longer ignore Redmond's strong, lean body, at least dancing with him occupied all her attention and left her none for brooding. No impossible thoughts of children or unpleasant images of women back home troubled her. There were just the two of them and the music, and after a moment she barely even noticed the irony of the song being played, with its wistful daydreamy quality underlying the insistent rhythm.

It was a song about if onlys. About the dreams that she'd just occasionally dared to dream as a teenager. The dreams she'd buried so deeply that for years it had never even crossed her mind to wonder why she wasn't interested in any of the pleasant young men who came through the dance school, tried to attract her attention, failed, and drifted off into the night.

It was an odd song, equally at home as a tough-talking tango and a gentle, wistful rumba. Redmond played with that quality, sliding a few slow swivels in among the tango's earthy rhythms. The complexity of the steps helped to settle her. There was no time to concentrate on anything except the moves and the music (he'd switched it onto an endless loop before joining her on the floor). Time slipped away, and Lisa was shocked when Redmond called a halt and she looked at her watch to discover that it was almost ten. She couldn't remember the last time an evening had flown by so quickly.

The tiredness hit her, as it always did, when she stopped moving. Sitting down to unbuckle her dance shoes, she wondered how she was ever going to get up again. A blister was forming on her left little toe, and she pulled off her sock and stuck a padded plaster over the sore spot. There would be plenty more of them before the competition, she was sure.

When she looked up, Redmond was gazing at her intently as if waiting for her attention.

"What?" She realised she'd sounded more snappish than she

meant to, but decided against apologising. Knowing her, she'd only make things worse.

"I hate to say this, but we really need to talk."

"Huh?" Lisa wasn't sure whether tiredness was making her stupid or Redmond was just making no sense. "Talk? Why?"

"The show. They're going to be in filming us any day now, and they're going to expect to find a couple. What if they ask us when we met? How we got together? We're going to need to have some sort of a story ready."

Lisa considered this. It was true. She wasn't sure why she hadn't thought of it before. Maybe she'd just been avoiding thinking about the idea of a relationship with Redmond any more than she had to. But she couldn't avoid it forever.

She capitulated with a sigh. "Tomorrow?"

"OK. How about we meet at your place?"

Lisa raised an eyebrow. So now he was inviting himself into her house. The one place where she'd thought she could retreat and gather her thoughts, safe from intrusive memories and daydreams. Trouble was, she couldn't think of a decent excuse to refuse. Oh well, maybe she didn't need one.

"Why not yours?"

Redmond grinned wolfishly. "Didn't think inviting you back to my hotel room would send quite the right signals."

Damn. She'd forgotten for the moment that he wasn't actually living back here. Just visiting. Long enough to turn her life upside down and send her crazy. Then he'd be back off to wherever he came from.

"OK, sixish at mine," she conceded, disdaining to respond to his predatory manner. "For dinner?" she added, in spite of her misgivings. If she had to start spending time with him, she might as well be hung for a sheep as a lamb.

Chapter 3

Lisa was making a final frantic attempt to hide the evidence of her scruffy and unsophisticated lifestyle when the doorbell rang. She shoved the last of the glass jars in the understairs cupboard and slammed the door, promising herself that she'd get around to putting the recycling out next week.

Then she hurried to the door.

Redmond was standing on the doorstep, uncharacteristically smart in trousers and a dark blazer.

"These are for you," he said, holding out an absurdly large red bouquet. As she took it from his hands, his fingers brushed hers, making her feel warm and fluttery.

It seemed odd that the slightest touch could have this effect on her outside the studio, when they spent so much time on the dance floor hand in hand, or even body to body, with his strong hands roaming over her bare back. Maybe it was the suggestion of romance that came with the flowers. Or the fact that she couldn't distract herself by concentrating on her footwork.

Oh God, why had she asked him here? His tall frame filled her doorway and she realised she was getting in the way. She stepped aside, but his hand caught her shoulder and held her in place as he leaned down to brush her cheek with his lips. His breath was warm and teasing on her skin as he pulled away, and for a moment she caught herself imagining how it would feel if he kissed her properly, his lips insistently seeking hers and his arms pressing her close, disregarding the flowers crushed between their bodies.

She hoped that in the dim light of the corridor he couldn't see her blush as he released her and she stepped back to let him past.

"In case anyone's looking." He grinned.

Of course. They were supposed to be going out, after all. She'd have to get used to this. Keep reminding herself it didn't mean anything. The flowers were a nice touch, though, and finding a vase and putting them in water allowed her to keep her back to Redmond until the blush had faded.

When she turned back to him, he was leaning in the kitchen doorway. Without her high-heeled dance shoes on, she had to look up a long way to find his face. When she did, his eyes were fixed intently on her. Her cheeks prickled as if threatening another blushing fit, but she refused to look away, intimidated.

"Do you want a drink?" she asked. The invitation was intended to sound casual but she suspected it just came out brusque.

"What is there? Better make it something soft—I came by car."

That surprised her. As a teenager, Redmond had cycled everywhere and insisted that running a car was a sin against the environment. She supposed it was living in America that had changed him, since it seemed that everyone there drove everywhere, but couldn't think of a way of making the comment that didn't sound confrontational.

Something in her expression must have given away her thought, though, or perhaps he'd just anticipated it, because he went on to explain, "Don't worry, it's not mine! The friend who it belongs to is away at the moment, so I've got the use of it. I can see how you could get used to having one, though."

"I wouldn't know," Lisa said over her shoulder as she bent down to get the bread out of the oven. "I've never had the chance to—can't afford to run a car and even if I could, it wouldn't be much use with the amount of traffic round here. Buses are easier."

She'd said it so often she almost believed it, but now she wondered. Had she just been listening to the echoes of Redmond's disapproving remarks all these years? Would it have made a difference to her opinion of cars if she'd been able to picture him easing through traffic behind the wheel of a sleek sports car?

Oh, why did he have to come back and stir things up? Life on her own might not have been pleasant but it had been simple. Nobody to make her think about why she made the decisions she made. Nobody to make her acutely self-conscious about the mismatched plates and glasses she'd inherited with the flat and never bothered to replace.

Glasses… that reminded her…

"So what are you drinking?"

"I wondered when you'd get back to that." Even without looking, Lisa could tell Redmond was grinning. She could hear it in his voice. He probably thought she was a scatter-brained idiot. Or else he realised it was just the effect he had on her. She didn't know which would be worse.

"You could have reminded me." She knew she sounded like a petulant child, but sometimes he was so infuriating. If he wanted a drink, why couldn't he have just asked for one?

"I could, but where would be the fun in that? Besides, you looked as if you had your hands full."

She couldn't deny that. Pasta had seemed like such a simple meal, but the addition of little touches like the warmed bread and fresh basil had upset her routine and now she seemed to be trying to do everything at once.

"Can I give you a hand with anything?" Redmond asked. She looked up from slicing the bread. She was all ready with a sharp remark if his expression was in any way patronising, but for once it was all seriousness.

"Why don't you pour yourself a drink?"

Redmond obligingly poured apple juice for himself and a glass of wine for Lisa. He seemed thoroughly at home in her small flat—so much so that she wished she could pretend he was just there as a friend. But he wasn't, and the complicated truth had to be confronted.

"So," she began determinedly as she set the pasta on the table. "About this programme."

Redmond waved a silencing hand.

"Let's enjoy dinner first. Shame to distract ourselves from it when you've gone to so much trouble."

"It's no trouble," she said dismissively, although a treacherous part of her mind reminded her that she wouldn't normally have been at the supermarket so late the night before, and that when she cooked pasta for herself it usually came without all the trimmings. And as for when she'd last turned the oven on…

Yes, well, she answered herself back, she didn't often have guests, so when she did it was nice to push the boat out a bit.

There was a pause, during which Redmond looked quite happy concentrating on his food, but Lisa felt awkward, sure that the sound of her chewing had suddenly become very loud. She wished she'd thought to put some music on, but now she didn't like to suggest it. Music and dinner was too much of a suggestive combination. What with the roses Redmond had brought, all it needed now was a few candles.

"So what brings you back to England?" she asked, hoping that the banal topic of conversation would dispel the romantic images that had crept into her mind.

A frown crossed his face.

"Sorry, shouldn't I have asked?" Now she felt guilty. "I don't mean to be nosy."

"No, it's a fair question. A few things. Partly business and partly personal. And it's been a long time since I was here last."

"You don't say." Lisa knew she was being sarcastic but it seemed safer than touching on the other aspects of his answer. He was obviously being deliberately vague. She didn't know if he was sparing her feelings or his, and she wasn't sure she wanted to find out.

He either didn't notice or didn't mind the sarcasm. His eyes were distant and thoughtful.

"We were such kids when I left."

Lisa didn't remember it that way.

"Twenty is hardly a kid. You seemed pretty grown up to me. And I'm sure you wouldn't have taken kindly to anyone calling you a child then."

"True." He grinned. "We thought we were so grown up." And then he shook his head in bewilderment at the thought. "I had no idea!"

Lisa laughed. It was true. She'd been so convinced that she knew everything. And she had known some things. The important ones. Like the fact that she'd needed to enjoy that last summer because things might never be so perfect again. Dancing and Redmond and what seemed like endless sunshine. What else could compare?

It seemed such a long time ago and, remembering that summer, a thought struck her.

"Have I changed?" She hadn't noticed much change in him, apart from superficial things like the driving, and a slight thickening around the shoulders. What did he see in her now? Was she different to the teenager he'd left behind so long ago?

"You don't look a day older. Right answer?" He was laughing at her again, but his warm laugh was so infectious it was impossible to help joining in.

"Be serious!"

"Okay, you look a little bit older and ever so much better. More confident. You look like someone who can take care of herself. Will that do?"

Lisa thought about it and decided that it would. It was certainly true. The year on her own, even more than her time with Brandon, had toughened her, though nothing since had hardened her quite so much as the first day she'd woken up knowing that Redmond was gone, not just for the summer, but for good. And now he was back and it was already beginning to seem as if all the time in between was just a hazy dream, or should it be nightmare?

"You're looking very thoughtful." Redmond studied her face

as if by looking hard enough he could ascertain the subject of her thoughts.

"Not really," she lied. She didn't want to tell him she'd been thinking how very easily she could get used to having him back. "The wine must be going to my head more than I thought. Making simple things seem complicated. I was just wondering what we should do about dessert."

"Have some?" he suggested helpfully.

"Ha, very ha." That was something Lisa hadn't said for years, though it had been trotted out at regular intervals when they'd been dancing together. Even then, she remembered, she'd bitten back laughter a dozen times a day, not wanting to show how easily he brightened up a dull practise session or a stuffy social event.

Funny that in all these years she'd never thought to wonder if things could have been different if she'd admitted quite how much he meant to her. Would he have stayed? Maybe if she'd begged or pleaded, but she wasn't the begging type. And besides, what if he'd gone away and left her feeling not only abandoned but also doubly a fool?

No, better this way. He was a good dancing partner, but that was all. And he was bound to have a girl in America by now. In fact, there was the small matter of those phone calls, and the letters she'd seen him stuffing into his pocket as they left the café. Definitely a woman's writing—she didn't know how you could tell, but you could.

Redmond was staring at her, and after a moment it came back to her that she was supposed to be fetching dessert.

She did so, although moving in a straight line to the fridge required some concentration.

"What did you put in that wine?"

"Just a drop of seventy percent proof. Why do you ask?"

She stared, aghast, then realised he was joking.

"You bastard!" She took a swing at him, intentionally missing but unintentionally sending his glass of apple juice flying. She grabbed a cloth and began mopping the drenched table. Her cheeks were burning with embarrassment at her clumsiness, but thankfully the action allowed her to turn her head away until the worst of the blush subsided.

"What?" Redmond demanded. "You knew I wouldn't really. Didn't you?"

Now he sounded worried.

Lisa considered this for a moment. Had she really thought he would spike her drink? She supposed not. Redmond was unpredictable, a bit of a joker, but he was basically a decent guy. If she'd thought otherwise, she wouldn't have given him a second thought after he left.

"Well, not once I thought about it."

"I should hope not." For a moment he sounded stern. Then he went on in a gentler voice, "You should know I would never do anything to hurt you."

It was on the tip of her tongue to say bitterly, "Except leave me." If she'd had even half a glass of wine more, the words might have burst out instead of melting away on her tongue.

As it was, there was an awkward pause, and then Redmond began again in a more everyday tone, "If you've finished, we'd better get on with thinking up a story while you're still sober enough to remember it once we've agreed on it."

"If I'm not, it will be your fault," Lisa snapped back automatically. Half her mind was still mulling over his comment about not doing anything to hurt her. It almost sounded like the remark of someone who cared. If he meant it, then was it possible that he didn't know how his leaving had hurt her? Not to mention the unanswered letters and the way he'd disappeared without leaving an address, so that for years her only news of him had been scraped together from gossip on the dancing circuit.

If he hadn't known he was hurting her, did that make it better or worse? It was hard to believe he could be so completely unaware of her feelings, so insensitive to the love that had always been the core of her life. But if he hadn't seen it, how could she blame him, when she'd fought so hard to hide it?

Maybe, she thought with a faint flutter of hope, she'd been equally blind. Could there be another reason for his leaving? Maybe it wasn't because he didn't care. But travelling halfway across the world from someone and ignoring her for years because you cared about her... what kind of sense did that make?

If only Redmond wasn't such a mystery. Sometimes she longed to just come out and ask him, but it wasn't the kind of thing you did, and certainly not when you had a dancing competition to think about. It was something to say when it all came to an end and if she made a fool of herself she wouldn't have to spend hours the next day in his arms or gazing into his eyes.

It was a question for another time.

Right now, the question, as Redmond was saying, was what they were going to answer to all the standard "couple" questions the TV crew were bound to ask. Redmond pulled out a pen and paper and began listing questions with ruthless efficiency.

How long have you known each other?

How did you meet?

When did you start dancing together?

When did you first realise you were going to be more than just dancing partners?

Where did you have your first kiss, and what was it like?

What are your plans for the future? Marriage? A family?

That one made Lisa wince inwardly. She'd never thought of Redmond as the marrying type. He seemed so restless and footloose. But the picture of him at home with a child in his arms suddenly seemed strangely believable. Had he changed? Or had Lisa been misreading him all this time? Or was she fooling herself now? Maybe the answer to the question was going to be, "Not in a million years."

Redmond chewed thoughtfully on the end of his pen. "Any more?"

None Lisa would dare to ask.

"Let's start with those for now," she suggested. "We can always add more later."

"Okay. I guess the trick is to keep as close as possible to the truth. We met at school. I took up dancing when a knee injury kept me out of football for a term. We were paired up by our teachers and never looked back."

"Were we going out together before you went to the States?"

Redmond thought about it.

"Maybe not going out. Too many questions about why I went. We were always close but we only started going out when I got back into the country."

"Three days ago? Won't that look a bit suspicious—we already knew about the programme by then."

"I've been back a week," Redmond said, looking deeply injured. "You mean you haven't been counting the days?"

"Time flies when you're having fun," Lisa countered.

"But if all I've been is fun…" Redmond picked up the song as she'd half expected him to. She'd always enjoyed the way he sang along to his favourite dancing tunes, but she'd forgotten quite what a strong voice he had. His rich tenor carried her along for a moment on a wave of melody, so that when he trailed off, she had to think hard to recall what they had been talking about.

"So we've been together for a week?" Lisa hoped she didn't sound wistful.

"I don't know. That doesn't really make us sound much of a couple. Maybe we should say it's a bit longer."

"That would be hard when we were in different countries. I suppose we don't have to tell them you've only just come back to England, but it wouldn't be hard for them to check up on."

"What about if we got back in touch recently and I came back because we decided we wanted to be together?"

The marketer in Lisa recognised a good selling story, and that was definitely one.

"I like it." She nodded approval. "How did we get back in touch?"

"Internet? That's common enough to be believable."

"Not bad. Childhood friends reunited on Internet find love. It has mileage." Lisa thought for a moment. "So who contacted whom?"

"Oh, I know. I saw you on FriendsReunited. Something about your job. You didn't even mention dancing. I only knew you were still dancing because I saw your bio on the teachers' page of Mark and Elaine's site."

Lisa was childishly pleased that Redmond had been taking notice of her career. Although how come he hadn't been in touch? Surely it wouldn't have been too hard to find her email address or get her phone number off Elaine. Mind you, it wasn't as if she'd made much effort to get in touch with him since college. After he hadn't answered any of her letters that first year, she'd written it off and tried to move on. Only now he was back did she realise how little it had actually worked.

That wasn't something she wanted to think about now. Better to concentrate on the details of the story.

"So, you found me on the web and got back in touch. By email?"

"How about by letter and phone? Less traceable."

"I'd still have letters."

"You'd have kept them? How sweet. Well, we can always write some now."

"They won't be postmarked with the right date."

"So you threw the envelopes away."

"Anyone who knows me would believe that?"

"You save envelopes?" Redmond stared at her as if she'd just admitted to being abducted by Martians.

In answer, Lisa got up and went to the bureau. Tucked in between the *Little House on the Prairie* books and *The Technique of Ballroom Dancing* was a shoebox. She shuffled it carefully out and carried it over to the sofa, setting it down with all the reverence you would accord to a holy relic.

Redmond came over to look as she lifted the lid.

Inside was a pile of paper and a thin stack of envelopes. She lifted out the envelopes and read off the postmarks. "5th May, Prague. 6th July, Malta. 20th August, Sicily. 30th September, Tenerife. That was the last one."

Redmond looked at her intently as if seeing her for the first time. She found her heart was beating fast as she waited to see what he would say about the letters which told the story of his first summer away from her – the only summer when she'd truly believed he meant to return. She'd intended to ask him whether he recognised the place-names, but his expression told her what she needed to know.

She felt as if she was walking on ice, the ground cracking perilously around her.

"What else have you got in that box?" he asked eventually. The cracking stopped. Safe from confrontation, she felt weak-kneed with relief, yet obscurely disappointed. Maybe she'd been trying to stir things up, get everything out into the open, ask why he'd left as he had, and why the letters had suddenly stopped.

Instead, she'd opened herself up a little, and got nothing in return.

That was the way it always was with Redmond. He gave when you were least expecting it, but when you wanted something you got nothing, or else a wholly unexpected response. Sometimes she wondered if he was doing it on purpose. Did he know what she was looking for and take pleasure in frustrating her?

As she mused, her fingers had been riffling through the pile of papers. Competition programmes, newspaper cuttings and photographs, carefully preserved in date order. She'd reached the one she was looking for, and pulled it gently out of the stack and placed it on the chair arm for Redmond to see.

"The President's Cup," he said, recognising the line-up that had been photographed for the local paper. Redmond and Lisa, looking much younger but not so very much different, beamed at a point just to the right of the camera. Redmond's mother had taken this picture, sneaking up behind the official event photographer. It was the first time his parents had been to watch him in a competition and Lisa had never been sure whether their presence had spurred him on to his first truly brilliant performance, or whether it had just somehow been his day.

"Remember the mad German couple?" he asked now, and Lisa nodded, laughing.

"Do you really think they were trying to sabotage us?" she asked, remembering how they'd repeatedly found themselves being halted or redirected as the tall blonde couple paused in the most inconvenient places or swept into a corner where Redmond and Lisa were posing.

She could still remember the sheer venom in Redmond's voice when he spoke of them after leaving the floor. It had frightened her a little. The memory of it still did. He was not a man to cross lightly, which might be part of the reason she trod so lightly around the subject of his desertion.

Redmond gave a dismissive shrug. "Probably not. It was just a lousy routine, which happened to conflict with ours and mysteriously reinvented itself whenever I changed ours to avoid them. Anyway, so what? We still won."

The crazy Germans had gone out in the quarterfinals.

Of the other couples in the photo, four had stayed on the circuit for some time. Two of them were still around, and one of the girls (now with a different partner) was rumoured to be in the running for the *Couples* trophy.

The fifth had vanished not long after the competition. That happened to some dancers. Life got in the way. Jobs, kids. You gave up a lot to take the competition seriously. Lisa had never regretted doing it for the few years she had. She wished she could have carried on for longer.

"Have you ever regretted becoming a dancer?" Lisa asked impulsively.

"What do you mean? Why would I?"

"I don't know." Now she'd asked the question, she wasn't sure why she had. What was there to regret? She considered. "The time. The work."

"It's not really work, though, is it?"

That made Lisa smile. Of course, she realised. That was why Redmond was so different from her other partners. Even fun-loving Jerry took dancing seriously. Redmond liked to win, but he loved to dance. Even on a bad day, he never quite lost the effervescence that came from dancing for the sheer joy of it. In a funny way, when you were doing it for love, mistakes mattered less, but excellence mattered more. Doing things right just felt so much more satisfying.

"What?" Redmond had noticed her smile.

"Nothing," she said, smiling even more. In spite of all the complications of the situation, it was good to have her favourite partner back. She must remember to appreciate it, because who knew how long it would last?

"Why does nothing make you smile?" His exaggerated expression of bewilderment made her laugh still more.

"Why should anything make me smile?" she threw back through her laughter.

"Why shouldn't it?"

She had no answer to that, so she gave up and went back to leafing through the cuttings.

Soon they were engrossed in memories of the different competitions they'd entered. The easy wins, the unexpected triumphs, and the occasional ignominious disasters. She still cringed at the recollection of the time her dress had split almost to the waist partway through a jive final. Although Redmond had maintained that the extra glimpse of thigh had distracted one of the middle-aged male judges away from the particularly perfect finale given by another couple, and moved Lisa and Redmond up a place in the final.

Then there was the time they'd ducked outside to avoid the heat of a stuffy sports hall without air conditioning on a summer evening, and almost missed the prize giving. They'd realised their mistake halfway through a rumba in the car park, and raced back in, panting, as the judge was calling their number for the third time.

And the time that, after an unexceptional performance in the Tango, they'd scraped into the final, and the music had started, unexpectedly blaring a pop single that Lisa had listened to a million times that summer. Knowing the song, they'd both sprung into life and danced better than ever before, working in such perfect tandem that Redmond had felt confident enough to adjust their routine a little, fitting it to the phrasing of the music and throwing in a bit of acting to suit the lyrics. On its own, that wouldn't have cut any ice with the judges, but the audience loved it, and their applause spurred Lisa and Redmond onto an even more perfect performance.

It was after that evening that Redmond had been approached by a dancer from London with the invitation to spend a summer on the cruise ships. A summer from which he'd only returned eight years later...

They'd spent so little time together, it seemed impossible that there could be so many memories.

The conversation lulled for a moment and Lisa made the

mistake of looking up to meet Redmond's eyes. It was something that happened a lot on the dance floor, from a distance, where the magnetic force of his gaze could draw her towards him without any deliberate effort on his part. At this close range, it was overwhelming. She could see the perfection of every lash, and the slight unlikely flecks of grey that softened the blue irises like mist over the sea on an autumn morning.

She looked away, but not before she'd seen the slight smile forming on his lips.

Now it was her turn to ask. "What?"

"If we carry on like this, we won't have any trouble convincing the TV crew we're a real couple."

"What do you mean?" she asked numbly. She'd been a fool to think there was anything going on, other than the effort to claim a place in the competition and a chance to walk away with the money. Her friends at work would say she should take advantage of it anyway. A fling was better than nothing, wasn't it? But Lisa knew it would make things worse in the long run. A taste of those full lips, a night beside that warm, strong body, and her life would seem even more bland and bare than it did already. She'd already had happiness given to her and snatched away, and she couldn't bear it to happen a second time.

Safe. It was a crazy concept, applied to someone as darkly, dangerously sexy as Redmond. Yet, somehow, impossibly, she did feel safe with him. Time and time again she'd let down her defences, began enjoying his company and their shared memories. And then, just when she was relaxing and enjoying the view, the cliff edge would crumble under her feet and she'd find herself leaping back from the abyss.

"Shared memories. Isn't that the essence of a good relationship?"

"It is?" Lisa looked at him blankly. She wasn't sure it was, but she definitely wasn't capable of articulating why that was wrong, or what was the perfect basis for a relationship if that was not.

"So I read in some trashy women's magazine."

"You were reading a women's magazine?"

Redmond grinned at her shock. She had the impression he enjoyed confounding her expectations. "Hospital waiting rooms are fascinating places."

"You were in hospital? You were ill?"

Somehow the idea of Redmond, with his robust healthy glow, in the sterile environment of a hospital, seemed wrong. She belatedly registered that she should have sounded more sympathetic, and was about to try to counter her blunder, but Redmond was already answering.

"I was at the hospital. I wasn't ill. A friend had some health problems and I took her in a few times for tests, so I got to sit and read until the doctors had finished with her. Sometimes it took a while."

Lisa suppressed a surge of jealousy for the woman who'd had Redmond sitting waiting for her when she emerged from the ward, jubilant or distraught. Lisa had always driven herself to and from hospital appointments, and she'd long since given up trying to share her few scares. People worried, or didn't know what to say, or brought the subject up later when you least wanted to be reminded of it. It was easier to do it alone. So why did she envy Redmond's friend so fiercely?

"That was kind of you," she said blandly, forcing her mouth to smile in denial of the storm that was raging inside. How come other people got someone to support them and she'd had to do everything alone? After her father's death in an accident, and even more during her mother's long illness and decline, there had never been anyone to look after Lisa. If anything, she'd been the one to do the looking after. Maybe that was why she'd kept her own collection of joys and successes so diligently. There was no one else to do it for her.

She put the lid back on the shoebox and set it down beside the sofa.

Redmond nodded. "That's plenty for one night. Don't you think?"

"I guess so. We can worry about the details later. At least we're agreed on a story."

"I'm almost looking forward to the auditions," Redmond said brightly. "It should be quite a show, not just taking on Fritz and Kathrin and all the rest, but pretending to be a couple for the benefit of the TV crew."

Lisa raised her eyebrows. He'd echoed her thought from the first time they danced together after his return. They were performers, both of them. They loved a show. She supposed that was why, in spite of all the tension, they got on so well.

Lisa never knew why she said what she said next.

"Wouldn't it be easier if we didn't have to pretend?"

Chapter 4

Redmond stared at Lisa for a long moment and she couldn't read his expression. She wished she could swallow the words back, but they were spoken and a lump of tension was forming in her throat. Then he began lifting his hand slowly. She watched, mesmerised, almost feeling the heat of his hand before it reached her cheek. Her mind ran ahead of the reality, seeing his strong fingers cupping her face and drawing her into the kiss she'd found herself daydreaming about earlier.

Even as she imagined his hungry lips on hers and the familiar warmth of his body close against her, the cautious, hurt part of her mind was warning her not to believe it. There was no future. With his job in America and his footloose, fancy-free ways, she was bound to get hurt. Still, she did nothing to stop him as he ran his fingers gently down from her cheekbone to her chin and turned her face towards him. Despite the heat of his touch, it sent a shiver through her.

She looked up at him then, and the seriousness she saw in his eyes threw a cloud across the sunlight of her imagined happiness. How had she ever thought he would even consider her suggestion? This wasn't a real romance, a fairy-tale ending for her. It was a cynical business ploy, a sham and a lie, and if she took part in it, she deserved every bit of misery it brought her. And yet, she'd known from the first moment that she couldn't refuse, if it bought her another chance to dance with her perfect, infuriating dream of a partner from long ago.

"Lisa," he said slowly, and even though there was a distance in his voice as he prepared himself to let her down, her name on his lips sounded sweet and sensuous, shaped slowly like a caress.

"I hate to turn a beautiful woman down, but life is going to be complicated enough as it is. Rushing into things for real wouldn't make it any easier in the long run."

As rejections went, it was a kind one, but it still stung.

"Rushing into things?" Lisa's voice wobbled dangerously. She swallowed hard, past the lump in her throat, and began again. "I'd hardly call it that. How long have we known each other?"

"Nearly ten years," he answered, and for some reason the fact that he knew the answer without thinking reassured Lisa a little. "But we haven't been in touch for most of that time. I think we've got some catching up to do before we get into anything serious."

Lisa already regretted her rash suggestion, and now that she saw an opportunity to backtrack, she grabbed it with both hands.

"I wasn't suggesting anything serious," she hastened to correct his impression. "More a... what do you call it... relationship of convenience. That's it." Surely that was something the worldly women he'd been used to wouldn't have a problem with.

"A relationship of convenience?" Redmond rolled the words around in his mouth with an expression that looked suspiciously like amusement. "Something to think about," he conceded. "But not tonight—it's getting late and we need to be fresh for the auditions tomorrow."

"Auditions?" Lisa squeaked, feeling sillier by the minute. Why had she assumed they'd just walk into a place on the show? There were dozens of other great couples on the scene at the moment, and some of them were even husband-and-wife partnerships. Lisa had never envied them before, but she did now. They'd have it so easy—no lies, no stories to keep straight, just being themselves and getting on with their lives. Not only that, but she envied them their lives. The evening with Redmond had given her a taste of how pleasant domesticity could be, when you were with someone who understood.

Brandon had never understood her dancing. He'd always said he thought it was a nice hobby for her to have, but behind that he'd been jealous and suspicious, too, of the time she spent with her dancing partners. If Jerry hadn't been gay, she suspected that her relationship with Brandon would have been even more short-lived. After Brandon, she'd vowed she'd only ever date dancers. Preferably good ones. It narrowed the pool somewhat, though, which was why she'd been single for a while now. Single and bored. At least the bored part was changing.

"So," she reined her rambling thoughts in, "when and where?"

Back on business, they made their arrangements quickly, and then, with a grin and a peck on the cheek, Redmond was gone.

*

Lisa couldn't get the day off work for the auditions—Gary was still keeping her busy with mailshot mock-ups—so she had to rush home an hour early, as soon as she escaped from yet another lengthy phone call to discuss the images, which he still wasn't happy with. She seemed to be getting more and more behind with the day job, and finally she'd broken one of her own rules and grabbed a pile of correspondence from her in-tray to take home with her. Maybe one night she'd actually get five minutes to do some catching up at home or the studio. She supposed she should have asked Redmond to pick her up from the office and bring her home, to save the bus ride, but she hadn't been keen on having him hang around while she got ready. Just having him in the house set her nerves tingling, and she needed all her concentration for this. What had possessed her to join in with this crazy scheme?

Elaine and Mark, of course. Not that they'd pushed her. If they had, she wouldn't have done it. But they were so desperate for something to save the studio, she couldn't have lived with herself if she hadn't tried. And she had to admit there was something in it for her too. With Jerry's accident, she'd have been partnerless and adrift, marking time until his injury healed, instead of competing alongside someone who was, at least on the dance floor, the perfect partner.

It was only off the dance floor that he left her floundering, as he did this time by arriving miraculously early, while she was still deliberating which dress was most suitable for the occasion. She'd narrowed the list down to three: the classic flirty little black dress, a short moss-green jersey wrap dress which brought out the fresh green of her eyes, and a striking claret number with a pencil skirt which perfectly showed off the figure she'd honed through hours of dancing and the occasional run and swim. Mercifully, she'd just stepped into the green one when the doorbell rang, so she abandoned the others in a heap on the bed, promising herself she'd take care of them later.

Lisa rushed downstairs, almost turning her ankle as her high-heeled shoe caught on the edge of a stair.

"Is this OK?" she asked, giving him a twirl.

"Not bad," he said, his eyes dancing. She guessed that meant good. "Will I do?" he asked in return.

He was wearing dark trousers and a soft shirt that matched his eyes and made them look even more intense than usual. It was a pity they wouldn't be dancing—it was the kind of fabric that screamed for you to run your hands over it, savouring the softness of the fabric against the masculine hardness of his body.

Oh God, why did he have to pick this moment to unleash the full power of his smouldering looks, just when she needed total concentration to deal with the crazy situation in which she found herself?

"Fine. Can you hang on while I do my makeup?" she asked.

"You don't need make-up," he said dismissively, but she chose to ignore him. She might not need it normally, but this was TV, and in her PR work she'd seen enough perfectly normal people rendered pallid and drawn by unfortunate lighting and camera angles to know that if there was a chance of ending up in front of the camera, she did need it.

"Wait there," she said, ignoring his impatience, and rushed upstairs.

By the time she'd finished smoothing on foundation and applying blusher in the right places, her emotions had calmed too. Now there was just the quietness that spread through her before a competition, when she knew that there was nothing more she could do; this moment was it.

"Ready?" she asked, descending the stairs more carefully this time.

Redmond jumped from the sofa with a guilty air, but she could see nothing displaced.

"Sorry, I hope you haven't been too bored," she said, hoping to elicit some hint of what he'd been doing, but nothing was forthcoming.

"No, I'm fine. We'd better go." He led the way out of the door and walked round to open the car door for her while she locked up the house.

"Doesn't it have central locking?" It looked like the kind of car that would. Big and black and sleek and powerful. Too much bonnet for the amount of body it had. A car that showed off, perhaps even more than Redmond himself did, even on the dance floor. It might be borrowed, but it suited him perfectly.

"Yes. That's no substitute for manners, though."

He waited patiently as she slid herself awkwardly into the low bucket seat, and wondered when he'd become so courteous. She supposed he was practising the devoted boyfriend act for later.

When she was settled, he closed the door gently and walked round to the driver's side.

"Sorry if I'm a bit quiet while we're driving," he said as he started the ignition. "I'm not used to the London traffic yet."

"I don't think anyone ever gets used to the London traffic," said Lisa, who was still smarting from her last attempt to cycle across London. She'd rapidly concluded that it was taking her life in her hands, and gone back to catching buses. It wasn't as if she needed the exercise with all the dancing she did.

"Not a big fan of London, then?" he asked, sounding surprised. "I thought you must love it here, you've stayed for so long."

Lisa thought about it.

"I don't know. I love some things about it, and hate others. But I think that would be true of anywhere. I've never really wanted to leave. And anyway, where would I go?"

"Anywhere. The country. The seaside. Abroad." He checked over his shoulder before manoeuvring out into the busy street. "France. Spain. America."

"America?"

She couldn't imagine herself there. What you saw of America on TV was a strange, alien place, with cities so large they seemed like entire worlds in themselves, and huge rolling plains. The scale was so different. She'd feel dwarfed, lost. Or so she imagined. Maybe that wasn't what it was like at all.

"Why not?" He grinned. "You could come out to Florida. At least we don't get rained on so often. You should at least come and visit."

Was that an invitation? Did she want it to be? A few months of Redmond merging into her life here was one thing, but what would it be like to be cast adrift in a foreign country with no point of contact except him?

"I'll think about it," she said, while trying to think about anything else except that.

Then there was a quiet spell while Redmond concentrated on the road.

Lisa left him to it, and listened to the music coming from the car speakers. The tune sounded faintly familiar but she couldn't think what it was. Something they'd danced to at some point, perhaps. There were few danceable songs they hadn't, and this song had the lively rippling rhythm of a perfect quickstep.

"Is this the radio or a CD?" she asked, when the road seemed to have quieted down a bit. She nodded towards the stereo.

"CD," Redmond answered. "I'm supposed to be choreographing something for one of my junior couples to this tune, and I haven't had much time to work on it. They need to start learning the routine next time I'm over there, so I thought I'd bring the album over here and start planning it. Haven't had much of a chance yet. Oh, and once that's done, the next in the pile is for an advert I'm choreographing."

"Busy, busy."

"Always." He nodded, smiled, and turned his attention back to the road. For all he'd claimed unfamiliarity with the London roads, he seemed perfectly in control, slipping smoothly from lane to lane, apparently confident of his direction. Lisa presumed he remembered the roads from his younger days, and this was confirmed when he tutted in annoyance at a no entry sign.

"That's become one way since I was last here," he grumbled, turning right instead and beginning a complicated detour.

"Here we go," he said at last, pulling up outside the big boxy building that housed the TV studio. "Why don't you go and sign us in while I find somewhere to park."

"I don't mind coming with you."

"And walking back here in those heels?"

"Hmm." He had a point. "OK."

Lisa got out and took the stairs as gracefully as she could in the impossible shoes, conscious of his eyes following her in the mirror until she was inside the building.

He gave a jaunty wave and drove off. Lisa frowned, suddenly conscious that he knew she was watching him. Mind you, that meant he was watching her too, so it was silly to feel embarrassed.

She turned to the reception desk, where two perfectly groomed twenty-somethings in navy designer suits made her feel suddenly gauche. How did they do that? Was it the perfect expressionlessness of their' faces (definitely botoxed, she concluded) or their unbelievable thinness and the way their cheekbones slanted prominently over their perfectly white-toothed smiles? Or the uncanny way they looked like clones of each other apart from the different shades of perfectly sprayed hair? She fought the urge to smooth down her already unrumpled dress.

"Redmond Carrington and Lisa Darby, for *Couples*," she said curtly, drawing on her own extensive experience of being a crisply professional receptionist. Had she ever been as scary as this? Surely not!

Redmond joined her as she was waiting for the receptionist to announce their arrival. He walked calmly but determinedly up the steps without a hint of the fluttery nervousness that Lisa was feeling. How did he do it? He'd probably look exactly the same if he was walking up the steps of Buckingham Palace.

"Please, take a seat. Mr. Weatherill is expecting you, and he'll be ready for you shortly."

Lisa stalked over to the huge leather sofa and perched herself on the edge. It was the kind of seat made for sinking into, wearing comfortable clothes, in front of a log fire. In her silky dress, Lisa couldn't get any grip on it, and if she sat back in her short skirt, she was sure she'd end up showing her legs right up to her underwear. Not that Lisa was shy—years of quick-changes behind the stands at amateur competitions had gradually eroded her modesty— but she couldn't bear to look so undignified in front of the two immaculate receptionists.

Redmond settled beside her, sinking comfortably into the corner of the huge sofa. Not for the first time, she envied him— and all men—his easy, practical clothing.

"OK?" Redmond asked, as if he sensed her awkwardness.

She nodded mutely, not trusting her voice.

"Not a bad office. I could get used to working here," Redmond said, looking round with wide, amused eyes. "Did you see the drinks machine?"

She hadn't seen anything except the icy gaze of the perfect receptionists.

"Seven flavours of tea including Earl Grey. The drinks probably come out in bone china cups," he joked.

Lisa's splutter of laughter echoed embarrassingly in the quiet hallway. She bit her lip and pressed herself more tightly against the arm of the sofa. Below the hem of her short skirt, the leather was cool against her legs.

As she looked around, she felt a warm hand steal into hers and give her a gentle squeeze.

She looked up, and saw Red's eyes dance with amusement. Of course, it was all part of the game. Look like the perfect couple. If anyone asks the receptionists, they'll say those two couldn't keep their hands off each other even in reception.

Pity. The reassurance would have been welcome, if it had been real. The feeling was still nice, though. She smiled back up at him for the benefit of the receptionists. Out of the corner of her eye she watched them exchanging whispers. Most unprofessional. She hoped it was because they were suitably jealous.

After a minute or two the blonder of the two receptionists stood.

"Mr. Carrington and Miss Darby," she said in that perfectly accent-free English that receptionists everywhere have to a fine art. Lisa wondered if she could still produce it on demand. She had a suspicion that if you'd been a receptionist once, it never quite disappeared.

Redmond stood, releasing his grip on her. Suddenly she found she didn't know what to do with her hand. It felt cool and conspicuous. She picked up her bag and fiddled with her shoulder strap, then realised it made her look nervous and dropped her hand to her side.

"Please follow me," the receptionist said crisply.

Lisa went ahead of Redmond, her heels clacking on the marble floor. She found herself falling into step with the receptionist, like a soldier marching behind his commanding officer, and forced herself to break the rhythm. It was surprisingly difficult, like dancing an off-time waltz once you'd learned to do it right. She was grateful when Redmond caught up with her and took her hand again, keeping her close to him so that her step now fell in time with his. That felt right, like dancing with him. Something familiar to fall back on in these intimidating surroundings.

They walked silently down a long corridor lined with still photos—some famous faces and others Lisa didn't recognise. There were small, neat captions under the pictures, but there wasn't time to read them. Maybe they'd get to look on the way back.

Finally the receptionist paused outside a big black door indistinguishable from all the others, and tapped on the door.

"Come," barked a voice from inside, and Lisa stifled a giggle. He sounded so much the stereotypical movie director she expected him to be sitting in a canvas chair with his title printed on the back, and smoking an oversized cigar.

The door wasn't open far enough to see in, but Lisa could see the receptionist's demeanour change from cool arrogance to an attitude of pure subservience. She had to admire the girl's versatility.

Her newly deferent voice was so quiet Lisa didn't hear what she said, but she certainly heard the answer.

"Show them in."

"Mr. Weatherill will see you now," the girl said unnecessarily.

Lisa wondered how having someone to speak for you had become a sign of rank. What was the point? It just doubled the amount of time everything took, and people were always saying time was money. But maybe that was the point. She made a mental note to mention the question to Redmond later.

Though, having seen Mr. Weatherill, she realised that she was going to have trouble remembering anything by the end of their interview. Far from the fusty old gentleman the surroundings had led her to expect, he was not much older than Redmond, with a black suit that cost more than the average competition prize fund, and looks that wouldn't have been out of place on a film star. She hoped that the way her eyes were fixed on him looked like polite interest rather than the wary fascination she actually felt. She hadn't thought men like this existed, at least not without copious assistance from makeup, wardrobe, and good camera angles.

She supposed he was the male equivalent of the scary secretaries. It must be something about a place like this. Maybe, she caught herself thinking for a moment, if she spent enough time here the effect would rub off on her. But who did she think she was kidding? It would just make her feel duller and dowdier than she already did. All the same, it was nice to have someone so stunning fixing an attentive gaze on her and welcoming her to the studios.

"Thank you," she said, a little breathlessly. Nerves, she told herself, not wanting to think about the alternative. Not since the day Redmond first swept her across a dance floor had she responded so physically to a man. And this was not the moment for that kind of complication.

Mercifully, Mr. Weatherill, who apparently preferred to be called by his Christian name, Tim, but couldn't persuade the secretaries to do so, turned his attention to Redmond. It appeared they had something in common—a keen interest in their local football team. Lisa hadn't even known Redmond still watched football, never mind that it was possible to follow their progress overseas through the delights of America's absurdly comprehensive sports channels.

Lisa found the game desperately dull and totally bewildering (she was sure the offside rule had been invented purely to ensure that she had no chance of ever comprehending what was happening during a match) but at least their small talk gave her time to calm down.

"So are you a fan too?" Tim asked, turning to Lisa with a smile that suggested he knew what the answer would be. She suspected that women in his world didn't do football, and for a moment she had an urge to disrupt his expectations by claiming a lifetime's devotion to the sport, but her position was already confusing enough without a further selection of unnecessary lies to sustain.

Instead, she opted for borrowing an easy story from Marion at work.

"Not likely. The footie gives me a chance to catch up with the girls—do some shopping or watch a DVD."

Lisa shopped only when she had to and couldn't remember the last time she'd got away from work and dancing long enough to watch a film from beginning to end (although she did occasionally catch bits of one on TV while doing the ironing). She hoped Tim wouldn't ask her about her taste in films, but fortunately he accepted the stereotypical response without surprise or apparent interest.

"That's nice." He nodded blandly. Thirty seconds' acquaintance was enough to prove that he wasn't as interesting as his appearance and setting had led Lisa to believe. Along with the relief that her life wasn't going to become still further complicated by an inconvenient attraction to the show's producer, Lisa also felt a flicker of disappointment. Where were all the fanciable men nowadays? The list of attractive men in her world seemed to have reduced itself to one candidate, and he wasn't interested. Maybe when the show was over she'd join an Internet dating agency. Then she remembered some of Terri's tales, before she'd met Dave and suddenly transformed into a perfectly sedate housewife and mother. Maybe not.

"So," Tim went on, his face suddenly flicking into serious mode, reminding Lisa of a moody black-and-white magazine image, "tell me why you two want to be on the programme."

Redmond and Lisa looked at each other. They hadn't prepared an answer for this, although in retrospect it was the most obvious thing for the programme makers to ask. It was like a job interview, wasn't it? You wanted to establish motivations, to understand whether you were going to fit together. And Lisa had been so busy thinking about the fit between her and Redmond (she fought back an image of their bodies intertwined) that she hadn't given a thought to how they'd fit in with the programme.

Finally they both began talking at once.

"You first." She nodded to Redmond.

"No, you," he shot back with a satisfied smile, knowing that she would capitulate rather than appear to be arguing in front of the producer.

"I was going to say two things," said Lisa, who had no idea what she'd been going to say. "For one thing, I never turn down a chance to dance. For another..." She paused, uncertain whether to mention the practical reason of the dance school needing the money, or the other more personal reason. She knew that mentioning wanting to dance with Redmond would win them points in the cute couple stakes, but for some reason she choked on the words. She faltered, and began again. "For the school..."

Before she could dredge up the remainder of her failed sentence, Redmond came to her rescue, launching into the story of how Elaine and Mark had approached them to ask them to dance. Cleverly, without lying, he gave the impression that they'd been approached as a couple rather than individually. He talked about the publicity that the show would offer the school, and the chance of an investor coming forward, as well as their hope that they would win and the prize fund would allow them to save the building.

Lisa found herself just a little disappointed. Even though she knew she shouldn't, she'd hoped against all reason that he would mention something about dancing with her. She wouldn't have believed that was the reason, of course, but it would be nice to hear flattering words come from his mouth. Later, in the quiet of her own home, she would replay them and let herself dream, just a little, about what her life would be like if they were true.

"So you're doing it for the school?" Tim asked. He didn't sound terribly interested. It was more as if he was just checking that he'd got his facts straight. His voice had the deadpan quality of a newsreader and she found herself wishing she could say something to evoke the life she'd seen there earlier, when the two guys were talking about football.

Before she could think of anything to say, Redmond had already jumped in.

"Well, that and the chance to spend some more time dancing with the most beautiful woman I've ever met." Redmond gave his dazzling, outrageous liar's smile.

If he'd said the prettiest, Lisa might have believed him. On a good day, with nicely coordinated clothes, a gently lipsticked smile, and her long brown hair brushed out, she knew she could be pretty. But beautiful? Compared to all the tanned model-types Redmond must see every day in America? That was a joke, and she knew it. In the midst of her pain, though, she had to admire his acting ability. Even knowing better, she'd thought for a moment she caught the ring of sincerity in his tone, and now he was turning his gaze on her as if he was admiring a precious work of art.

She wished that just once in her life a man would look at her that way and mean it. Not just as if he admired the way her body moved on the dance floor, but as if he could see past it to her soul.

Well, until this programme was over, there was no chance of anyone else looking at her that way. Redmond and work and dancing would leave no room in her life for anyone else, and besides, who else was there? The only men in her life for months had been sweet, gay Jerry and slimy ad-man Gary. No, she might as well face it, she was stuck with admiring Redmond from a not-altogether-safe distance for the foreseeable future.

And then what?

At some point he'd go back to America and they'd have to tell the world something about how the supposed romance had ended.

Just fizzled out? Somehow she couldn't believe that. More likely he would storm off in a row. Or she'd just wake up one morning and find him gone. The thought still stung, more than it should, and it preoccupied her throughout the rest of the audition. What would happen once the show was over?

She asked Redmond about it later in the car.

"Will we ever tell people the truth about us?"

"What truth?"

Redmond's eyes were firmly fixed on the road and his jaw was set tight. She wished she hadn't said anything. It was too big a conversation to have while negotiating the London traffic, but she'd needed to know. Would she have to spend the rest of her life maintaining a lie?

"That we're not really going out."

She hoped it didn't show how hard it was to get the words out.

A frown flickered across Redmond's face and now she wished even more that she hadn't pushed the issue, but it was too late to back down.

"Depends."

"On what?" She wasn't sure she wanted to know, but the question was out of her mouth before she could stop it.

Redmond shrugged and opened his mouth to say something, and then out of nowhere a car shot out into the road in front of them.

He slammed on the brakes and they lurched to a halt just inches from the offending vehicle.

Redmond swore under his breath and carefully put on the handbrake and sat for a moment while the other car pulled away, the driver waving a jaunty hand in thanks and blithely ignoring how close he had come to disaster.

"Idiot," Lisa murmured with the vehemence usually accorded to much stronger language.

Redmond slowly moved off again. "Some people." He shook his head.

The previous conversation was apparently forgotten and Lisa didn't quite dare bring it up again. They drove in silence for a while and then Redmond asked casually, "So, how do you think it went?"

She hated questions like that. They made her feel as if she was in an exam, knowing there was a right answer but unable to select one from the many possible options. For everything she could have said, she could see a reason why it might be the wrong response.

Finally she shrugged and said lightly, "OK, I suppose. You think they'll pick us?"

"I think so," he said, surprisingly confidently. Mind you, that was the attitude with which he'd always approached life. Things would work out—why shouldn't they?

Lisa wished she had his faith.

Chapter 5

"I wonder who'll be here," Lisa remarked idly as they started up the studio steps. She'd been hoping ever since Redmond texted with the details of the first show that they wouldn't see too much of the Barbie doll receptionists. She wanted to meet the other dancers, and see what the competition was like.

"You haven't been reading the message boards, then?" Red asked.

"When would I have had time?"

"At work, maybe, I don't know."

"I should be so lucky." Lisa remembered guiltily the letters that were still sitting unanswered at the bottom of her handbag. She wouldn't be spending time browsing on the Internet until she'd dealt with the pile of correspondence, and that didn't look like getting done any time soon. In the meantime, she'd just have to rely on second-hand information. "So, I take it you have."

"Yes. There's quite a bit of talk about who's going to be on."

"And?" Lisa could have sworn Redmond was deliberately stringing out the time before he told her anything, just as the commentators did when announcing the results on dance programmes.

"The boards seem quite definite about four of the couples. Fritz and Kathrin."

Lisa nodded. She'd expected that. They were one of the most established couples on the British scene, even though neither of them had been born here. She'd come over from Switzerland, and he from Germany, and they'd paired up in their teens and never looked back.

"David and Caroline." Of course. A married couple with their own studio, they could hardly have been omitted, but Lisa didn't consider them serious competition. Their presence simply meant one couple less to worry about beating.

"Harry and Tiffany." Lisa grimaced at that. They were stunning dancers, but Tiffany had a reputation for temperament. Her presence would make for good TV, but it was bound to ensure that the competition was anything but a smooth ride.

"Al and Eveline." Al was an easygoing American. He'd met Lancashire-born Eveline at an international festival and, to everyone's astonishment, moved to England to be with her as fast as he could quit his job and find a flat in Blackpool. They were a cute couple, and among the more serious contenders, especially on the Latin side.

"It's anybody's guess for the other two places. Except of course that we know we've got one of them. So it's just the sixth couple that we really don't know about."

"And I think we've just found out." Lisa nodded to the couple standing just inside the main entrance. They were already dressed and made up, even though it was over an hour before anything was due to happen.

"Oh, hell," Red breathed.

"My thoughts exactly."

Xander and Kasia Lebowitz were exactly as over the top as their names suggested. They were stunning performers and technically flawless, and they'd wiped the floor with Britain's top couples over and over again in the first few years after Red left for the States. There had been a collective sigh of relief when they'd retired for Kasia to have their first child, and there had never been any signs of their return. Now it appeared they were back, with a vengeance.

"Well, that's going to set the cat among the pigeons. No wonder they didn't want us to see the lists in advance." To Lisa's amazement, Red let out a deep, throaty laugh. "I can't wait to see Tiffany's face!"

And in spite of herself, Lisa joined in the laughter as she followed him through the door.

*

Lisa been doing her own dancing makeup for years and had got it down to a fine art, but apparently TV was a whole new game, and they weren't going to trust it to an amateur, no matter how experienced. As soon as they were inside, Red and Lisa were whisked off to be coloured and powdered and costumed, and they didn't see each other again until they were led into the studio to line up on couches in front of the cameras. Men were on one side, looking sober in their tail suits with just a flash of colour from the bow tie and cummerbund they'd been given to match the girls' dresses. There they would remain until the couples were called forward, one by one, for their first moment in the spotlight.

Seated on the other side with the girls, Lisa felt like a hummingbird amid an array of tropical flowers, surrounded by the bright colours of all the ballroom dresses. She, like most of the girls, was wearing a dress she'd been given by the wardrobe department, but she noticed that Tiffany wasn't in the same sweeping halter-necked dress with matching sleeves, but in a longer, fuller dress with a two-tone skirt and diamante bodice. Trust Tiffany to get special treatment.

"Everybody ready?" Tim called breezily when all the seats were filled except the presenter's spot right in the middle.

"OK. Let's have a big hand for our fabulous presenter, Phillipa Morris!"

Dutiful applause.

It was the first time Lisa had seen the presenter anywhere except on the cover of *TV Times*, and she didn't quite know what to expect. Phillipa seemed pleasant enough, Lisa decided, as she came in, joked with the dancers, and explained that the show would be filmed in two parts. Today there would be the introductions, so the audience knew who to cheer for, and the dancers would get to know the judges who would be deciding, each week of the show, who would stay and who would leave. Then tomorrow all the dancers would get together to prepare their first-round dances, and a group number. Each week after that, there would be a live show, including clips filmed during the week at the various practice venues. Finally, having checked that everyone understood the rules, Phillipa went on to announce that tomorrow's filming would include both their first-round dance, a quickstep, and a group rock'n'roll number to an Elvis medley.

Lisa grinned at Red across the room. They producers weren't doing things by halves. She supposed with only six couples in the contest, and five weeks from the introduction to the grand final, they needed to get the big show-stopping numbers in early. Lisa liked rock and roll. She figured they were going to have fun.

"So, without further ado, it's ON WITH THE SHOW!" Phillipa declaimed, and suddenly there was a hush as all the people who'd been bustling in the background melted away. Only the presenter, camera crew, and lad with the clapperboard remained.

The filming of the first half seemed to Lisa to pass in a blur. She tried to concentrate on what was being said about the other couples, and then, when she and Red were called up, to give intelligent answers to the presenter's predictable questions: "So where did you two meet? Are you looking forward to the competition? What would it mean to you to win?" All the time, her heart was hammering and she seemed to be waiting for someone to ask, "What do you think you're doing? Liars! Frauds!" Maybe it would be better when they started dancing.

But there was another long night to get through in between.

*

"OK?" Red caught Lisa in the corridor as they left the studio after the filming.

She nodded numbly.

"I thought it went well. Didn't you? It was fun finding out about everyone. I never knew Fritz used to be a climber, did you?"

"No." Even though all she'd done was sit on a sofa for an hour, Lisa was suddenly exhausted from the excitement and worry, and she wanted nothing more than to go to sleep.

"Are you sure you're OK?" Red asked, putting an arm around her shoulders and drawing her to one side while the other couples walked past them, chatting and laughing.

"Just tired," she said, and after a moment's hesitation, she relaxed against him, letting her head sink onto his shoulder. Red turned towards her, leaning over her protectively and stroking her hair, and for a moment Lisa could feel again what it would be like to be loved and protected by a man like him.

What a shame it was never going to happen.

She let herself enjoy the feeling for a moment longer, and then took a deep breath and stood up straight.

"Come on, let's go and get ready. Where are we going after this?"

"My place."

Lisa looked at him blankly.

"Did I miss something? I thought you were in a hotel."

"Not anymore. I thought it would look a bit weird if I was staying in a hotel rather than with you, so I've got an apartment—just a short-term let. So we'll have to get used to the whole 'my place or yours' thing now."

Lisa supposed she should be polite and congratulate him on having a new home—or at least a new place to stay—but her pleasure for him was overtaken by a flood of annoyance that he'd sorted it all out, not only without involving her, but also without even telling her.

"What if someone had said something today? How do you think it would have looked if I hadn't even known where you were staying? Don't you ever think?"

"Hey," Red soothed, putting his arm around her again and walking on so that she had to fall into step beside him. "No squabbling in public. I'll tell you all about it in the car on the way there, how about that? And we can stop at yours to pick up some clothes and night stuff if you like."

He sounded like a parent humouring a cross child, and Lisa wasn't impressed, but she had to concede the need for a united front in public. For all that she wasn't elated about the idea of losing the small amount of private time she ever had at home, Redmond did have a point. It'd look pretty weird if they never spent the night together. That just wasn't a prospect she wanted to think about right now.

"OK." She wriggled out of his grip and fled for the dressing room.

Opening the door, she was greeted with an enthusiastic shriek.

"Lisa!" Tiffany exclaimed with an exaggerated pretence at delight. She fluttered her fingers in a wave, which flaunted her huge engagement ring. Lisa was sure it was deliberate. "So good to see you again. I had no idea you and Red were an item. You'll have to tell me all about it!"

In your dreams, Lisa thought. She wasn't about to start pretending to be best friends with the horrible woman just because they shared a dressing room.

"Sure," she said reluctantly, since she couldn't think of any excuse to refuse outright. "But I have to rush tonight. Red's not long back from America, so we could use an early night." Lisa gave a broad grin, inviting Tiffany to form her own interpretation of what they'd be doing when they got home.

Caroline turned from where she was unfastening her huge clip earrings.

"I'm glad for you," she said quietly, giving Lisa's shoulder a squeeze. "I hope you'll be happy."

Where Lisa had been strong in the face of Tiffany's veiled hostility, she was nearly undone by Caroline's kindness. A tear prickled the corner of Lisa's eye, and she hastily brushed it away with the back of her hand.

"Thanks," she said. "It's good to see you. I'm so glad you and David are in the show."

Lisa meant it. They provided a welcome note of sanity and everyday friendliness in what looked likely to become a hotbed of seething jealousies before the first show was over.

Caroline smiled back and returned to removing her makeup. Lisa did the same, trying to avoid catching anyone's eye. The less she said, the less chance there was of letting anything slip that she shouldn't.

Before too long, the room started emptying, and Lisa made it out to the foyer without exchanging more than a casual word or two with the other dancers.

It was a relief to find Redmond waiting for her, chatting with David. Like her, he seemed to have gravitated towards the friendly, unchallenging participants, and tried to steer clear of the incipient rivalry and bitterness.

"Ready?" Red asked, when he saw Lisa approaching, and when she nodded, he excused himself from his conversation and led her out to the car park.

"Come on, let's get home," he said, throwing their costume bags in the boot.

"Home?" Lisa was surprised that he was already referring to his flat that way. She'd been a year or two in hers before she'd started thinking of it as home.

"Well, it's as much of a home as I have for the next six weeks. I might as well get used to it."

"True."

Redmond already knew his way to Lisa's flat, and after a brief pause there for her to grab a bag and some essentials, it was on to his new home. Red's place turned out to be in a trendy south bank apartment block. It was exactly the sort of polished wood and chrome bachelor pad Lisa would have picked if she'd been asked to imagine Red's ideal apartment.

"Very nice," she commented. By the standards of that sort of place, it was. It had a jacuzzi bath and built-in cinema system and, she was relieved to see, a roomy spare bedroom. All in all, he could have done worse. It felt like a very expensive hotel. It just didn't feel like home.

"You think? I think it's a bit soulless, but the agent found it for me and I didn't have a lot of time to spend on house hunting. It's only for six weeks. But it's hardly Rosie's cottage, is it?

Lisa still remembered the gorgeous seaside cottage that she and Redmond had once stopped at on the way back from a dancing competition, so that they could grab brunch with his pretty cousin at her home. Lisa's dominant memory of the occasion now was Rosie's chubby and domineering ginger tomcat, and she laughed as she imagined its reaction to being deposited in this gleaming pile in place of its usual cosy surroundings.

Then the laugh turned into a yawn.

Redmond took the hint.

"You must be exhausted. We'll talk more in the morning."

And, even though Lisa knew there was a lot to talk about, with plans for their dances the next day and for the week ahead, she happily agreed. Tomorrow would be soon enough for all that.

*

Lisa slept late, and Red only woke her when it was close to time to leave for a long day's practice and filming, so she found herself swept through breakfast, makeup, and wardrobe, and onto the dance floor, without ever having taken the conversation any further. Standing in front of Redmond as the music was about to play for their first heat dance, she couldn't help letting her eyes wander to the other couples on the floor.

The competition was daunting, but no worse than she and Red had handled in the past. In those days, though, they'd danced together day in, day out for months. This time, their renewed partnership was barely more than a week old. Oh, and there was the small matter of the lies they were telling just to be in the competition at all. She felt a sinking in her stomach every time she remembered the hideous, embarrassing moment when she'd set herself up for rejection. Why had she ever suggested that they should stop pretending?

Even though she'd backtracked and pretended she'd only meant a relationship of convenience, she had the feeling that Redmond had seen into her heart and uncovered the sudden longing there… and that he hadn't cared.

Faced with this new rejection, there was only one thing to do. What Lisa had done all her life in good times and in bad, and done overwhelmingly better than anything else: dance.

As if on cue, there was a drum roll leading into the brisk beat of a quickstep and the eight couples began their progress around the huge dance floor. Even with all the couples on the floor, there was all the space in the world for Lisa and Red to sweep across the centre of the floor. The designer dress had been practically sewn onto Lisa, the cerise satin clinging to every hint of a curve. She'd made the mistake of wishing out loud that she'd lost a few pounds for the show, and Red had laughed at her. The video footage would be the acid test, she supposed, if she could bear to watch it. Probably Red would make her, so that they could analyse the competition and dissect their strengths and weaknesses.

She watched them now, surreptitiously, out of the corner of her eye, as Red whisked her from the familiar combinations of locks and runs, into an open American-style move fresh from his Florida studio. Without his sturdy body looming in front of her, it was easy to let her eyes skim from the glittering duo of Fritz and Kathrin, flicking their legs in a rapid crackerjack in one corner, to David whisking Caroline's tall, elegant form along one edge of the floor.

Those two couples were serious competition, she thought. Her practised eye confirmed that the Braithwaites were, as she'd expected, solid and reliable. They were good teachers too, whose appearance on the show would, if the stress didn't erode their sense of togetherness, bring a new stream of students to the Midlands studio which was making a small reputation already as the greenhouse to a new generation of movers and shakers. But they were better teachers than they were performers, and their presence was more due to their reputation as one of the longer-lasting couples in the dance world, than to their talent or style.

As Tiffany and Harry paused in the centre of the floor to execute a stunning sequence of scissoring moves, Lisa grudgingly admitted to herself that they were closer competition than she would have liked. Lisa had never liked Tiffany, since the day she'd overheard her whining in the dressing room at Blackpool at their first major competition. Lisa had been awed and inspired by the whole event, even though she'd gone from being a leading light in her own small world to a very small sequin in a vast galaxy of glittering stars. It had been time for the next stage, and she'd welcomed the challenge. Tiffany, on the other hand, had complained about the facilities, her coach's decisions, her partner's choice of routine, and the other couples' behaviour on the dance floor.

But there was no sign of that truculence on her face now, as she completed her manoeuvre, hovered for a moment like a bird of prey about to dive, and then swept off in Harry's arms.

When the figure brought Lisa face to face with Red again, he hissed at her, "Focus." She felt like spitting angry words back at him. She knew her brief survey of the competition hadn't affected her dancing. Her feet had been flowing smoothly the whole time, and her expression of alert enjoyment had never altered. Only the slight movements of her eyes would have told a sharp observer that her attention was on anything other than synchronising her steps perfectly with Redmond's. And yet he'd noticed. Sometimes his powers of observation were quite uncanny.

As if in proof of this, as they paused in a graceful sway, he gave her fingers a quick squeeze. If an outsider caught the movement at all, they would take it as a gesture of affection, but Lisa knew what it meant. Red was reminding her. Stay in the dance. She didn't know how he even knew her mind was wandering. She took a slow breath, letting the gradual filling of her lungs coincide with her smooth shift back to an upright position ready to move off again.

Then she was back in the moment, moving in perfect unison with Redmond across a floor that might as well have been empty, because she was totally unaware of the other couples, of the purpose of the competition, of anything except their magical gliding on a carpet of music. She was buoyed up by the speed of the music, the lively beat, the smooth velvety tones of the singer, and the warmth of Red's strong arms surrounding her. These were the moments she lived for.

Then her focus was shaken by a glimpse of motion from the corner of her eye, somebody approaching them, closer than another dancer should be on such a vast floor. There was no time to brace herself for collision or move aside, only to gasp in shock as Tiffany and Harry changed direction and shot into her path, and then there was the dull pain of an elbow thudding into her jaw, followed almost instantly by the searing pain of a stiletto heel sinking, with the wearer's entire weight behind it, into her right instep.

Lisa heard herself let out a quiet cry as she stumbled and collapsed, her throbbing foot no longer able to support her. Red's arms tightened around her, bearing her weight as she put down her other foot and settled her weight onto it.

"Are you OK?" he asked, the look in his eyes turning the everyday enquiry into an expression of tenderness. It would be so easy to believe that look, and to melt into his protective embrace, but even for the cameras, she dared not let herself.

He's acting, she reminded herself every minute. And he was good at it. He was hanging on Lisa's answer as if the world depended on it, and she supposed that in a sense, their world did. If she was too injured to dance, there was no chance of them going forward in the competition, and no point in the whole painful charade.

Lisa swallowed hard and nodded. Tears had sprung to the corner of her eyes. Her jaw ached dully and her foot still felt the impression of Tiffany's heel, but she was more shocked than damaged. She slowly set her injured foot down, and found that, although still painful, it would support its share of her body weight.

It was only then that she thought to look around her to see how the collision had affected the other dancers. She'd expected to find Tiffany and Harry hovering nearby, perhaps nursing bruises themselves, and waiting to see if Lisa and Redmond were all right. But the space Lisa looked up into was empty, and it was only when her scanning gaze reached the far corner of the dance floor that she saw Harry and Tiffany blithely continuing with their routine. It almost looked as if they were unaware of the whole incident, except that when they spun so that Lisa caught a brief glimpse of Tiffany's face, her sharply outlined lips were creased into a cruel smile.

The uneasy feeling Lisa had developed when she realised who had cut into their path solidified into a certainty. The collision had been deliberate.

"Bitch," Lisa breathed, almost silently.

"Shh," Redmond silenced her. His eyes were no longer soft and kind, but hard and angry. "Don't ever say that. You can't prove it was deliberate."

"No, but I know it was." Lisa's voice rose to a hurt, angry wail and she winced as her slight movement, made without thought, started her foot throbbing again.

"It doesn't matter," he said quietly, his head bowed so that the cameras couldn't pick up the movement of his lips and he could have been murmuring tender words to his injured sweetheart. "You don't know when the cameras are on you. We don't say anything we can't prove, ever. It's only sinking to their level. You're better than that."

The compliment should have comforted her, but it just made her angry. It was only a way of making sure she did what he said, against all her own principles. She knew what Tiffany had done, and the horrible woman didn't deserve to get away with it. Redmond should have backed her up on that, but this wasn't the time or place to argue about it.

"Whatever," she said with a brisk shrug. "Let's dance."

"Can you?" The solicitous look was back, proving if proof were needed that it was all for her dancing, and not at all for her. To him she was a dancing mannequin, a human robot. That was all, but if it was all she was, she would do it well if it killed her.

"I'll have to, won't I?" she said, more sharply than she'd intended. It was so hard not to show her pain and anger, not just at the incident, but at his distance and his lack of support. This once, she supposed, it didn't matter. To him, the pain would seem to come from her aching foot and jaw, and the anger from Tiffany's deliberate sabotage of their routine. At least, that was what she told herself. It was the only way to get through the rest of the routine without tears.

Red's relief as she raised her arms back into ballroom hold was palpable.

As Lisa forced herself to swing out her damaged foot and step onto it, a tiny gasp escaped her lips, but within an instant her careful smile was back in place. The next step was easier, and the moment she was able to lift her sore foot she found a brief instant of relief, but then she had to step onto it again and again, and the fast pace of the dance jarred her over and over. There could only be a minute or so of the song left, but to Lisa it felt like a lifetime as she forced herself to follow the dancer's mantra: keep moving, keep smiling.

Mindful of Red's earlier instruction, she tried to let go of her anger and focus on her dancing, but it was hard to relax into the movement through her discomfort and the continual nervousness each time she saw another couple appear in her field of vision that their approach heralded another crash.

It was a huge relief when the music shifted from its regular beat to the drumroll that built to a final crescendo. Lisa and Redmond had practiced a pose for the ending but it relied on Lisa taking all her weight on her right foot. With a wry smile, Red led her instead into the mirror image of their practised move, and as the music cut off with a final dramatic chord, Lisa rested on her left foot and kicked her right leg high, pausing with her head thrown back for a long moment, and blessing Redmond's thoughtfulness, because holding her weight like this on her injured foot would have been agony.

Red signaled to her with the slightest shift of his body weight that it was time to drop the pose, and around them the other dancers too settled back to standing positions. Just when she'd expected to be hating Redmond and Tiffany in equal measure and never wanting to dance again, the audience, as if released from a spell, burst into applause, and despite her aches, Lisa felt on top of the world. In spite of Tiffany's attack and the stiff competition from Fritz, Kathrin, Harry, and the dreadful Tiffany, Lisa knew she and Red had handled the dance well. And a small part of her was glad to have the moral high ground over Harry and Tiffany.

But she knew the anger was still there inside, glowing like red coals ready to burst into flame again. Tiffany and Harry cheated.

And Redmond did nothing. He'd never looked more brilliant than he did right now, with his Florida tan still glowing against the crisp white collar of his dress shirt. He'd never danced better than he had today, leading her smoothly through both the practised parts of their routine, and the variations forced on them by Tiffany's antics. At this moment of bittersweet triumph, Lisa's love and admiration for him, which had faded into the background of her life for so long, fought their way to the fore. But the simmering anger mixed with these emotions felt very close to hate.

"That was a nasty bump," Phillipa was saying over the dying applause. "Let's go over to the two couples involved now, and make sure we don't need to call an ambulance."

She went first to Tiffany and Harry and, with a smile almost as unconvincing as Tiffany's, asked whether collisions were common in the quickstep, since things moved so fast.

Lisa thought that was a stupid question, but she forced herself not to let her lips shape the thoughts, even in an undertone. There were people out there, if not in the audience here then watching at home, who could lip-read.

"Of course accidents do happen," Tiffany murmured silkily, "but usually when somebody makes a mistake or is careless. If you plan your routine well and keep an eye on what other people are doing, you shouldn't clash often, and when you do, it's quite easy to just pick yourself up and keep on going."

Lisa seethed at the implication that it was Lisa and Redmond who had failed in their planning or observation. Tiffany and Harry had changed direction at the last possible moment, and there was simply no way she and Red could have compensated for such deliberate bad gamesmanship. Lisa drew in a sharp breath to protest, but before she could find the right words, or indeed any words, Red's hand lay restrainingly on her arm, and it was to him that Phillipa turned with a smooth smile.

"Well, it seems Harry and Tiffany have recovered well. Let's see how the other couple has survived the first incident of the show. Who knew dancing could be so dangerous?"

Redmond laughed his relaxed laugh, and Lisa fumed. It was easy for him to laugh. He wasn't the one who was aching from head to foot, with pain and injured pride and the indignity and injustice of it all.

"I was into football before I was into dance," Redmond confided to the presenter, and Lisa died a little more inside as she watched his gently flirtatious manner and realised that Phillipa was surely the kind of pretty, successful, confident woman Red would be attracted to in the real world. The only places where Redmond and Lisa belonged together were the dance floor, and her dreams.

Lisa could hardly bring herself to watch as Phillipa widened her eyes, obviously attracted to the thought of Redmond's athletic past. The blonde presenter made a small, appreciative noise, encouraging Redmond to continue. "And I can honestly say..." He paused a little, as if about to betray a revealing secret. "...there's very little to choose between them in terms of how tough and demanding they can be. We got unlucky today, but these things happen. I just hope there's no lasting harm done." His magnetic gaze transferred seamlessly from Phillipa to Lisa.

Lisa forced what she hoped was a brave smile. "Just some bruising, I think, but I should probably get it checked out after the show, just to be sure."

"Of course," Phillipa agreed glibly. "A dancer's feet are so important, you can't be too careful. And now, let's hear how some of our other competitors got on with their first group dance."

As Redmond had just done, she smoothly shifted her intense focus from Redmond and Lisa on to the next nearest couple, which happened to be the Braithwaites. "David and Caroline," she greeted them with a show of delight as if they were her new best friends, "how did you enjoy your quickstep?"

Like Redmond, Phillipa had the ability to make someone feel

like the centre of the universe for a moment, and then dismiss them without a second glance. Really, Lisa thought, looking from his dark chiseled good looks, to her statuesque blond form, they deserved each other. They'd probably get together after the series, once Red didn't have to pretend to be with Lisa any more. Lisa wondered idly how long they'd wait.

Chapter 6

This time, Tiffany didn't even wait to get to the dressing room before she started on Lisa.

As soon as the cameras stopped rolling, everyone started getting up from the sofa to go and change. Lisa paused for a moment, delaying the moment when she had to put more weight on her sore ankle.

It was a relief to see Redmond coming over. Not that there was much he could do to help, but somehow his presence was a reassurance.

Tiffany hadn't gone either.

"That was a nasty bump," she remarked, shifting a little closer to Lisa on the sofa, into the space that Caroline had vacated. "We were worried about you."

"Yes, you were obviously very concerned," Lisa remarked. "I presume that's why you waited around to make sure we were OK after running into us at full tilt. It's so nice to know someone cares."

"Really, Lisa," Tiffany didn't allow her smooth façade to crack for a moment, "we're professionals here. The show must go on, regardless of our personal feelings. I thought you'd know that. But then, of course, you've not been dancing much apart from teaching the kids' classes for the last few years, have you? I suppose one forgets these things."

One does? Tiffany's cut crystal accent and perfect diction could almost fool you into thinking she'd been born in Kensington rather than the East End, but Lisa had met football hooligans with more manners.

"I suppose one does," Lisa agreed icily. "Funny, I had a notion that it was professional to face up to the competition and take one's chances, instead of trying to sabotage anyone who might be a threat."

There was a long silence. Then Tiffany slowly drew in a breath, and was obviously ready to speak, when Redmond chimed in, "I'm sure you didn't mean that the way it sounded, Lisa. Is your ankle hurting very much? Maybe we should go and get it looked at. Here, lean on me."

And he swept Lisa off, her feet mercifully hardly touching the ground, while Tiffany stared after them as if she could shoot daggers of ice into Red's and Lisa's backs if she just tried hard enough.

"Ignore her," Red said.

"I can't. You try ignoring someone who launches a full-scale attack if you happen to stand in the wrong place. I never know what she's going to do next. We can't just let her get away with it."

"We can. We're better than them and they know it. That's what it's all about. All we have to do is keep going, and sooner or later they'll be out of the running."

"If she hasn't crippled me in the meantime."

Red sighed heavily as they turned the corner and arrived outside the dressing room. "I know it's hurting, but try not to overreact. It'll only stir up more trouble."

"And try not to patronise. It won't make me feel any better." Lisa lowered her voice to a hiss as she noticed an unfamiliar man standing outside the dressing room.

"Is Lisa in there?" he called.

"She's here," Redmond answered for her.

"Hi, I'm Jonathon, the physio. Can I get a look at that ankle?"

"Sure."

Red pulled up a chair for Lisa and she sat down. It seemed odd being examined in the corridor, but she supposed it saved disturbing the girls while they were changing.

She bit down hard on the whimper that tried to emerge when Jonathan manipulated her ankle.

"Does that hurt?"

Her wince answered for her, but she told him, "A bit."

Red was hovering over her protectively. Some protection he'd turned out. She wished he'd go away.

"Just a bit of bruising," Jonathon said. "Try some ice when you get home, and you might want to put a support on it for a few days. Take it gently, but don't stop moving altogether." Nothing Lisa hadn't expected.

"Thanks," she said. "I'll be fine now," she told him and Red, then dived for the dressing room door before they could argue. Inside, she flung herself down on her chair and fished in her bag for one of the range of supports that she knew would still be there from the other times she'd wrenched an ankle, knee, or shoulder.

By some miracle, the other girls seemed to know she needed to be left in peace, and got changed in almost complete silence. One by one, with a murmured, "Hope it feels better soon," they left, until Lisa was sitting alone in the empty room, staring at a blank wall bathed in cold white flourescent light, and trying to summon up the energy to move.

Finally, there was a tap on the door.

"Lisa? Are you still there?"

Redmond. Of course. How had she thought she'd get rid of him just by sitting it out? He'd probably been sitting outside the door all this time, watching the others leave.

"Yes."

"Can I come in?"

"OK."

Moving still seemed too much effort, and she sat slumped in her chair as the door creaked open.

"Need a hand?"

In the mirror, Lisa watched Redmond approach her chair. She didn't want to rely on him. He hadn't backed her up after the collision—if anything, he'd behaved as if she, not Tiffany, was the foolish one who needed to be humoured. He'd been helpful, true, but not exactly sympathetic. And he'd flirted with the presenter. She couldn't trust him. But if she didn't move soon, she'd still be sitting here when the caretaker came round to lock up. And she didn't feel like moving without a strong arm to lean on.

Lisa took the offered hand and levered herself to her feet. Red swung her bag onto his other shoulder, apparently unworried about being seen walking around the TV studio carrying a large and exceedingly pink leather holdall. Lisa couldn't help grinning at the effect.

"Let's get some dinner," Red suggested. Lisa wanted nothing more than to go home, soak in a warm bath, and hide under the covers. But now Red had mentioned food, she realised her stomach was ready to begin growling. There probably wasn't any food at home, and if there was, it would be well on its way to independent life.

Lisa didn't feel like going out. Plus, she'd just caught sight of herself in the mirror. She'd taken her hair down from its stern pleat, but it was so thick with hairspray that the waves had stayed in place, and now stuck out awkwardly in all directions. And Red had interrupted her before she'd removed her make-up, so she still had thick black lashes, green eyelids, and bright slashes of blusher across her cheeks.

"I'm a mess," she protested. "I can't go out like this. Why didn't you warn me?"

"Firstly, you're never a mess," Redmond said firmly, "and secondly, even if you are, you still look ten times better than most people when they're smart."

"That's not true and you know it. But it's nice of you to say so."

Lisa didn't remember him being so gallant. Was it something he'd picked up on the cruise ships, or in America, along with "Have a nice day"?

"It's entirely true."

Yes, and he probably said that to all the ugly old widows on the cruises too. She almost liked him better when he wasn't being charming. She knew where she stood with the affectionately teasing insults that had been part of their youthful friendship. She didn't quite know what to do with this smooth, adult new Redmond.

"But if it makes you feel any better," he went on, "the place I'm thinking of going, it really doesn't matter how you look."

He gave a mischievous grin and Lisa wondered what she'd let herself in for. McDonald's? Or a greasy spoon café?

"So, is that OK? Shall we go?"

"Go where?"

"You'll see. It's a great place." Of course it was. Eight years out of the city, and Redmond still knew the best places to eat. Just as on Friday evening, though, he was giving nothing away. He must have been told that girls liked to be surprised. Maybe someone should have explained that, now and again, it was actually nice to be treated like a partner in the relationship instead of having all the decisions taken for you.

Still, there wasn't much point in arguing about it now. Lisa simply didn't have the energy. Anywhere she could eat would do fine, and then she could head home to bed.

She watched curiously as they passed the shops and restaurants on the High Street and she eyed each eatery in turn, wondering what he had in mind.

"This way." He turned into the car park of McDonald's and she laughed nervously. Hungry as she was, burgers and chips weren't her idea of a good dinner, although she had to admit there was a certain nostalgic charm to the junk food of their teenage years.

"Remember how we used to get burgers to eat on the bus back from dancing?" she asked.

"How could I forget? Ah, the delicious greasiness of cheap buns soaked in beef fat."

"So we're not going to McDonald's then?"

"What do you take me for?" He laughed. "No, we're not going to McDonald's. This is just a short cut."

They emerged from the car park into a narrow street she'd never noticed before, and Redmond pulled up alongside the last space in a row of cars. He angled the car neatly into the space and then came around to help Lisa out.

She noticed a stylishly lettered board by the door of what she'd assumed to be just another small terraced house. Discreet bronzed script across the window of what looked like a front room told her that this was Marrakech. Sure enough, on closer inspection, it looked like a small piece of Morocco transplanted into London. The door was teracotta coloured, and the doorsill was tiled with an intricate abstract mosaic.

Lisa let Redmond hoist her out of the seat, but she was determined to make her own way to the door. She pulled away from Red as he moved to lock the car, and he reluctantly released her. Before she'd taken two steps, though, she somehow turned her shoe on the edge of a paving stone and found herself faltering.

Instantly, Redmond's strong arm was around her, steadying her.

The sudden unexpected warmth of his body against her startled her more than the fall had done, and she drew in her breath sharply.

"All right?"

She made the mistake of looking up and found herself dizzied by the intensity of his eyes on her.

Speechless, she nodded.

"Sure? We want you fit for dancing," he said, and she couldn't tell if he was joking or serious.

"I'm not Jerry. You can't get rid of me that easily." She forced herself to sound light and cheery. All that mattered was the dancing. Right. She could do that.

She drew herself up straight, forcing herself not to wince as she put her weight back on her sore foot. She'd already been told it wasn't seriously hurt, and suddenly she didn't want Redmond's strong, protective hand resting on her back a moment longer.

Redmond spread his hands in a mock-innocent gesture.

"Do I look as if I'm trying to get rid of you?"

Lisa shrugged. Sometimes she didn't know what he looked like. It was hard to tell what he was thinking when he'd switch from joke to serious in an instant and back again a second later. He could mean anything, or nothing.

"Is this where we're going?" she asked, gesturing towards the small café in an attempt to deflect the question with another of her own.

In answer, Redmond pushed open the door and ushered Lisa through.

She gasped. It was like walking into a tiny, exotic grotto. Low sofas clustered around small tables, with the odd small leather stool scattered around. Swathes of white cloth separated the deep, narrow room into a series of secluded booths, illuminated by soft coloured lights and candles. There was a scent of something spicy, and low music was playing.

"Wow," Lisa couldn't help murmuring.

Redmond grinned. She thought he was reacting to her expression until she noticed the small man who had seemingly drifted out of the shadows to greet them. Lisa found herself being helped out of her coat, relieved of her bag, and ushered to one of the sofas, where Redmond joined her, still exchanging muted small talk with the tiny man.

She hadn't been able to hear what they were saying, but when the man bent solicitously towards her to adjust the cushions around her, she caught a few words.

"…see you again, and your lovely guest. You have done well for yourself this time."

So this was where Redmond always brought his women. A slow fuse of anger began to burn in her.

"This is Lisa," Redmond introduced her. "Lisa, this is Luca, who owns the restaurant. He's also one of the finest chefs and best kept secrets in London."

"You will please keep the secret? It would not be so lovely if it were full of strangers. Here we are all friends. It is only to be shared with someone special."

Or a whole series of special someones, if you were Redmond, she supposed, although how he'd found the time to do so was beyond her.

Nonetheless, she nodded. Then, as Luca turned away, the anger flared into life. She didn't want to be just another in Redmond's string of women, and at that moment not even the thought of the dance studio and the TV crew could make her accept that as her place.

"And I'll let you into a secret in return, Luca," she said sweetly, and he drew close and listened hard, no doubt expecting to hear sweet murmurings about her wonderful Redmond. Well, he could think again. "Don't believe everything you hear. Redmond's nothing special. He's just a guy who dances and thinks he's God's gift to women. They're ten a penny."

Luca stood open-mouthed and even Lisa began to wonder what had possessed her. Of all the moments to drop her act and tell the truth, she'd done it in front of a gnome-like restaurant owner she'd known precisely two seconds! There was no telling what it could mean for Redmond and Lisa's attempt to pose as a couple. Though perhaps a lovers' tiff wasn't so unlikely. If the two of them were together for real, there would be plenty of them.

Of course, restauranteurs heard it all, and Luca soon recovered his composure and bustled off to find "something for the lady and gentleman to drink while they settle their differences."

"What was that for?" Redmond turned to her, looking more inquisitive than angry.

Lisa shrugged.

"Come on, you can tell me."

"I don't know."

How did you explain your irrational fury in one or two short sentences to someone who was sitting looking at you with such an open, reasonable expression? The truth was so complicated. She was suddenly furious with his arrogance and presumptuousness and with the whole stupid situation. Here she was pretending to be a person not in love with him pretending to be a person in love with him, when all the time the truth was that she was only angry because she wanted him so much it hurt.

She opened her mouth to try explaining, but no words arrived, and eventually she settled for reiterating, "I really don't know."

"You do," he insisted.

"Stop telling me what I do and don't know. You can't read my mind. If you could, you'd know why I was cross, wouldn't you?"

She was pleased with that masterstroke of logic.

"OK, I can't read your mind. So you'd better tell me, hadn't you?"

Lisa shook her head. The more she thought about it, the less she felt she could explain her outburst.

Redmond's eyes, fixed on her, were losing their gently inquisitive look. He was frowning now: an expression Lisa recognised well, although she wasn't sure she'd ever been on the receiving end of it herself. It meant an impending storm.

"You must have meant something." Redmond wasn't going to let it go.

Lisa would have to tell him something.

She racked her brains.

"Nothing much. I've had a lousy day and my ankle hurts and I was taking it out on you. I shouldn't have done that. I'm sorry." Somehow the apology failed to sound meaningful. Probably because she was still furious and didn't mean a word of it.

"Is that really all?" Redmond asked disbelievingly. The thundercloud dispersed as fast as it had arrived, but Redmond still looked at her intently, as if it would enable him to divine her thoughts.

"Yes," Lisa said, quietly but in a slightly defiant tone, daring him to suggest there was more.

The silence between them lengthened. Redmond didn't say he didn't believe her, but she knew it by the way he was waiting for her to speak again.

"No," she amended, confused. "Maybe. I don't know. Oh God, I don't know. Just stop it! Leave me alone!"

She sank her head into her hands to hide the tears that shamefully, hotly pricked her eyelids. She rarely cried, and when she did, she cried silently: streams of hot tears running down her cheeks and escaping through her fingers.

Somewhere in the distance she was aware of the gentle clunk of glasses being set down on the table in front of her, and Redmond's voice murmuring, "Thanks." Then she heard Luca's footsteps receding and Redmond's voice, closer now as he leaned in towards her, asking with a gentleness she'd never imagined him possessing, "What is it? Is there anything I can do?"

What could she say to that? The first answer that presented itself was, "Get out of my life," but he'd already done that for eight years and it hadn't helped. It was hard having him back, but she wouldn't wish him gone again. No, senselessly, despite her anger at being taken for one of his many women, that was exactly what she wanted. Well, not exactly. She wanted to be not one of many, but the one and only. She wanted him to care for her and protect her against the awful Tiffany, and all their opponents. Only Redmond wasn't that kind of man. Never would be. And Lisa had never thought she was that kind of girl.

Reluctantly, she concluded there was only one possible answer. "No. I'll be OK."

She swallowed hard and sniffed, and for a moment the tears stopped.

"You sure?" Gently, almost imperceptibly, there was a touch on the back of her neck. Slowly, smoothly, like a parent soothing a fretful child, Redmond ran his fingers across her hair. That finished her off. The tears were back, drenching her hands and dripping into her lap in huge splashes like raindrops onto the pavement on a hot summer night.

She couldn't have said afterwards how long they sat like that: her sobbing through her hands and Redmond caressing her hair. There seemed to be two sensations going on at once in her mind. The indescribable sweetness of his touch and the terrible sadness of feeling that this pitying gesture took him further from her than ever. What would he think of her after this inexplicable behaviour? Had she thrown away her chances of love, as well as success in the all-important competition? The thought brought more tears and she pressed her hands hard into her eyes to try and dam the flow.

"Lisa, what's the matter? Tell me."

His voice was soft and urgent and so persuasive that for a moment she had the urge to just collapse into his arms and confess all.

She shook her head. It was as much a statement to herself as to him. She couldn't, wouldn't, say a word until after the competition.

She swallowed hard, blinked again, and managed finally to force out the words, "Nothing, really. I just don't feel too good."

"Shall I take you home?" he asked, and now she managed to turn her tear-stained face upwards and meet his eyes.

"You don't need to come. I'll be OK." She sat upright abruptly, causing his hand to drop away from where it had been resting against her hair.

The place where it had been felt cold and empty, and the tears threatened to start again. Lisa forced them back by focusing her mind ruthlessly on external things: the colour of the light falling through the patterned glass lampshades onto the tables; the complicated patterns of the wood-grain and the weave of the sofa fabric.

There was a drink on the table: something cool and blue and enticing, like a swimming pool on a summer day. She vaguely remembered Luca putting it there.

She stretched out a hand for the drink, then regretted it. If she was this emotional beforehand, what would she be like after a potent cocktail? But her hand was already on its way, and the cocktail gave her something to focus on other than Redmond's bewildered expression and searching gaze. She kept her eyes on it as she clasped her fingers around the cool stem and lifted the glass to her lips.

It tasted sweet and fresh and innocent, but the burning sensation in the back of her throat told her all she needed to know. It was dangerous, but then, weren't all the best things? She took another sip and rolled it around her tongue, enjoying the explosion of flavour and the way it focused her attention. Suddenly the world seemed a far less worrying place.

"I thought you were going home," Redmond's voice intruded.

"I am. But it would be rude not to finish the drink now it's here," she made an excuse. She knew she should go, but somehow she seemed to have become rooted to the sofa. Just as long as Redmond knew it wasn't him she was staying for.

"I didn't get the impression that being considered rude mattered that much to you."

Lisa couldn't meet his eyes. She knew she'd behaved like an idiot, but could bring herself neither to apologise nor to explain.

"Anyway, if you're going to drink that, you should have something to eat. Otherwise you won't be safe going home."

Lisa acquiesced, sipping the smooth blue drink as Redmond somehow, without appearing to move or speak, summoned a spread of bread and oil and olives and plump rusty red sun-dried tomatoes. Once it arrived, she remembered how hungry she was. Her mouth watered as she watched Redmond tear off a chunk of bread, dip it until it glistened with oil, and hold it out to her. He offered it towards her mouth but she put out a hand to take it instead.

"You'll get oily," he pointed out, stopping her wrist with one hand as he deftly manoeuvred the bread to her lips.

She gave in gracefully, for once, and took it from his fingers. As her lips closed around the moist bread, a drop of oil escaped, tickling her skin lightly as it ran down her chin. She ran her tongue across her lips to catch the dripping oil, savouring the warmth of the bread in her mouth and the rich, nutty flavour of the oil on her tongue.

"You missed a bit," Redmond said, sounding smug. Lisa rolled her eyes. She could never do anything right where he was concerned. She didn't know why she didn't just give up and go home. Admittedly, cold ham and cucumber sandwiches on stale bread at the bare kitchen table weren't as appealing as a cosy little restaurant, fresh bread, olives, tomatoes, and cocktails, but at least she knew she wasn't going to fall out with anyone over the rather tired contents of her fridge.

"Stay there." Before she could say anything, Redmond had leaned in closer, brushed a finger across the offending trail of oil, and brought it away gleaming. Now her skin was clean but the feel of his touch lingered. Crossly, she ran the back of her hand across her face, scrubbing it clean of the last remnants of oil and at the same time erasing the memory of his fingers gently brushing her skin.

Redmond put his hand to his own mouth and licked off the oil from his fingertip. For a moment Lisa couldn't help imagining that it was her hand to his lips, his tongue teasingly caressing the sensitive whorls at the tips of her fingers. She dragged her gaze away and reached for her drink. It worked pretty well as a distraction, but it was going down fast. She'd really better have something else to eat with it.

Soon she was wolfing down the food while Redmond watched her with amused eyes.

"So, are you staying for dinner?"

She capitulated with a nod and a laugh.

"You sure you can bear to stay for dinner with me? I'm nothing special."

Lisa's words made her wince, especially as she recognised how untrue they were. How many other men would have taken her outburst in such good part? He was still here and still smiling, and even if the only reason for it was the arrogance that prevented him taking her criticisms seriously, that still made a difference. Not that she was going to say so. He was big-headed enough already.

"No, but the food's pretty special. If the appetisers are this good, I can't wait to see what the main course is like."

Redmond laughed, a wide-mouthed, deep, genuine laugh. It made Lisa want to join in, but she kept her face serious and gazed at him with wide, injured eyes. She didn't want to be laughed at, even if she knew she did deserve it, and even if a part of her was laughing too.

"What are you laughing at?" she demanded.

Redmond was saved from answering by the reappearance of Luca with menus and another two cocktails.

"Did we order those?" Lisa whispered when Luca's back was safely disappearing.

"No, but Luca knows what I like."

"Maybe so, but how does he know what I like?" she asked, anger rising in her again. She didn't like being treated like the standard companion. Just because Redmond always plied his women with cocktails didn't mean she wanted them. She had the urge to ask for something different just to prove her point, but the truth was it would be a shame to waste the cocktail. They were very tasty. Maybe she'd have something different next time.

"A lucky guess?" Redmond suggested, eyes gleaming. Lisa was beginning to suspect he was enjoying baiting her. "So, what do you fancy?" He leaned back in the deep sofa, legs folded, and opened the menu out, studying it ostentatiously, although Lisa suspected he didn't need to.

"What's good here?"

"I wouldn't presume to suggest what you'd like," Redmond said, adopting an injured tone in his turn.

Lisa sighed. She'd get no peace with him in this mood. She went back to studying the menu herself, but before she'd read a third of the way down the page, Luca was back, hovering expectantly.

"We haven't decided yet," Redmond said apologetically.

Lisa cut him off.

"I have," she contradicted, enjoying his surprise as she picked a dish at random and placed her order.

"The usual for me." Redmond smiled as if sharing a joke with the waiter.

Lisa was puzzled, but she wasn't about to ask. She took another sip of the cocktail and curled up in the corner of the sofa, hands twined around the stem of the glass.

Redmond turned towards her and looked her up and down.

"You look very much at home here."

"Meaning?"

"Just what I said. Does everything always have to mean something else?"

"Not always. You sounded as if you did, though."

"What made you think that?"

"What is this, twenty questions?"

Lisa realised that, without intending to, they'd slipped into a game of questions. Now that Red had pointed it out, she wasn't going to be the one to break the pattern. That would be too close to admitting defeat.

"Why would I want to play twenty questions?"

"Why wouldn't you?"

"Would it matter if I did?"

"Does it make a difference if it matters to me?"

"Why would it make a difference?"

By now Lisa was laughing delightedly as she recalled the many long waits between rounds of competitions that they'd whiled away like this.

"Can you think of a reason?"

Redmond was laughing too, and when Luca returned to lead them to a table he gave them a benevolent, fatherly smile.

"It is lovely to see the young lady smiling again, no?" he said, possibly to Redmond or possibly just to the world in general.

"It is. Doesn't she have a lovely smile?" Redmond slipped his arm proprietorially around her shoulders and Lisa, who wanted to squirm, was forced to continue smiling a fixed grin as Luca summoned his wife over to admire the lovely young couple.

Mercifully, they soon bustled off to fill the table with an artistic spread, and then the "lovely young couple" were left to enjoy their meal.

"What was that for?" Lisa hissed as soon as Luca and his wife were out of the way.

"We've just had a row. Look like you're enjoying making up, for goodness sake. Luca's a good friend—we can trust him—but there are plenty of other people in here. I can't put a gag on just because you're in an awkward mood."

"Me? Awkward? I can't believe that coming from the person who's done nothing but patronise me, contradict me, and make fun of me all evening."

"Hey, that's not fair. I've done nothing of the sort."

Lisa glared. That wasn't how it looked to her.

"I haven't," he protested. "If I did, I certainly didn't mean to! Come on, be nice and let's enjoy dinner now we're here."

Lisa's glare subsided fractionally but she wasn't ready to forgive and forget entirely.

She reached for her drink and Redmond leaned across the table and snared her hand.

"What's up with you tonight?" he said. "I've never seen you so prickly. Relax!"

He began stroking her hand, gently, his fingers playing across the back of her hand, then the palms, then digging gently into the tense muscles of her fingers. It felt good, but even as Lisa's body relaxed, her mind became more vigilant. Despite the loosening effect of the cocktail, she was on her guard. She didn't want to feel too comfortable with Redmond's new kind demeanour or with the casual physicality he'd begun displaying in public since they'd officially become "an item." She was used to being independent and on her own, and she didn't want that to change. What if she got used to being with Redmond, behaving like part of a couple, and then he took off again for America? Or, worse, brought his girl over here, so that she had to watch him do all the same things with someone else she'd come to expect him to do with her? That might possibly be her worst nightmare.

She let her hand lie limply in his and looked at the glass of sparkling mineral water, which Luca had placed on the table along with the main course. The bubbles rose slowly to the surface and disappeared with a pop.

"Are you going to let go of my hand so I can eat?" Lisa asked.

"You seem to be managing well enough," Redmond pointed out. She'd managed to scoff most of the bread sticks and salad left-handed, but the stew still sat untouched.

"I can't eat stew with one hand."

"You can. You just hold the fork in one hand and shovel it in."

"Shovel it in? How elegant!" Lisa looked unconvinced and eventually Red released her hand with a sigh and returned to his own dinner.

The silence stretched out between them until eventually, for something to say, Lisa asked how he knew of the restaurant.

"I used to work here."

Whatever Lisa had expected, it wasn't that. She couldn't imagine the sophisticated man in front of her as a subservient waiter, although that seemed more likely than scrubbing dishes or slicing vegetables out back.

"When?" He'd barely spent any time in this country, and as far as she knew he'd been at school, football, or dancing for the time he had been here.

"My second year of sixth form I worked here on Friday and Saturday nights."

Lisa mentally calculated. That meant he'd been working here when they started dancing together. How come she'd never realised? Friday practice had been early, and when he'd rushed off afterwards she's always assumed he was just going to the pub with his football mates. And Saturdays had been their one day off. So it was perfectly possible, but how strange that he'd never mentioned it.

"What else don't I know about you?" she asked flippantly.

Redmond gave the impression of thinking hard. It erased the smile lines at the corners of his mouth and somehow made his blue-grey eyes seem darker and smokier. For a moment she thought he was about to reveal some deep secret, but then the sparkle came back and he grinned broadly.

"I'm allergic to zucchini?"

"Ha, gotcha! I knew that. You told me at the service station on the way back from the competition at Sheffield, except that you called them courgettes then."

"So I did! How on earth did you remember that?"

Lisa shrugged. She could have said that she remembered a lot of silly things about him, that it was easier to remember a joke they'd laughed about ten years ago than what her boss had said to her yesterday. She said nothing.

Redmond assembled an arrangement of salad and rice on his plate with great concentration and then set about demolishing it.

Lisa gave up on the conversation and concentrated on scraping the last of the stew and rice off her plate. Then she served herself another helping, which made a nonsense of her intense concentration on clearing the plate.

Redmond either didn't notice, or felt he'd teased her enough for one day, because he said nothing.

Finally Lisa admitted defeat and pushed her plate away.

"I'm so full," she remarked.

"Not too full to dance, I hope," he replied.

"Dance? Why?" Lisa knew she looked blank and stupid, but she couldn't imagine why he was asking about dancing. They'd more than done their practice for the day, and the only other place you could dance at this time of night was a nightclub. They'd always agreed that there was no point dancing at clubs because there was never room to move properly and they both detested the loudness and the thick haze of smoke you always had to walk through to get in and out of the building.

"Shame to waste a good empty dance floor. That's if your foot's up to it now. Want to test it out?" Redmond gestured to something over her left shoulder. Lisa twisted around and saw for the first time that part of the restaurant had been left empty as a slightly raised dance floor. Behind the trailing vines there were even mirrors that would reflect the dancers, as well as making the small room look a little more spacious. Lisa was impressed with the design.

"Care to dance?" Redmond stood up and held a hand out to her.

As if on cue (and perhaps it was, because Luca seemed to notice everything) the light salsa beat that had been going on in the background turned up a notch. Lisa found her feet tapping, and she stood up, wobbling slightly.

"Too much of the Blue Lagoon?"

"No, it's just my ankle settling down. It's not too bad now I've got the support on, but it's a bit wobbly," Lisa said, though in truth she did think she'd drunk a bit too much to dance well. Not to mention eaten too much to dance energetically. She hoped the music would slow down a bit, because the song that was playing was very lively and as Redmond sent her onto the dance floor in front of him, she found it hard to keep up the pace.

Her feet soon settled into the rhythm, though, and she showed off some fancy footwork, keeping her back to him and watching his movements in the mirror as he approached her. She was ready for his hand on her shoulder spinning her back towards him and into his waiting arm. This time when he caught her around the shoulders and swung her downwards, her body relaxed into him of its own accord. He smiled down at her for a split second and then she was being flung back upwards. She caught his hand to steady herself and then she was off again, flying with the music. It felt good to dance just for fun again after all the serious work they'd been doing. And now that she was moving again, it was easy to ignore the slight dull ache in her ankle.

She soon forgot the other diners, her injuries, and everything but the dance, until the music ended and Redmond caught her in a dramatic pose. Applause broke out, rippling across the restaurant. Lisa remembered herself and smiled and bowed for the audience. Redmond stood to one side, directing the applause towards Lisa, and as she gestured back, deflecting responsibility to the man who was, after all, in charge, she realised that for once she meant it. She knew he made her dance a million times better, look a million times better. With Jerry and the two or three others she'd danced with since Redmond, she'd been the stronger half of the couple, but with Redmond she was perfectly matched.

She reached for his hand and drew him to centre stage to share the applause. He deserved it, she thought, smiling muzzily.

As if in answer to her earlier wish, the music began again, this time a slow, gentle rumba. Plenty of opportunity to get her breath back, although it was a difficult dance too in its own way. Redmond certainly wasn't out to make it easy for her. He began with their usual opening steps but soon abandoned them in favour of something she'd never done before. It wasn't a surprise that he'd picked up some new steps while he'd been away, but she hadn't expected him to throw them at her in front of a room full of people.

He must have seen her panic because as he drew her into a close hold he leaned towards her to whisper, "It's OK, just follow me. I won't do anything you can't keep up with. Trust me." And despite the number of times he'd hurt her, confused her, broken her heart, at that moment, in his arms, listening to his warm reassuring voice, she did.

She kept her eyes locked on his and her hand firm in his grasp and let him lead, and sure enough her feet followed easily as he led her through a complicated sequence that she suspected, if she'd let her eyes stray to the mirrors, would have looked perfectly stunning.

The music ended too soon for her, but Redmond timed it perfectly so that she was caught in his arms as the last note faded away.

There was a second of total silence as the music ended—the best accolade any performer can ask for, and one she'd experienced only a few times, and always with Redmond. In that short space of silence, he bent his head towards hers and as she looked up enquiringly he tightened his hold on her and brushed her lips with his. This time, under the spell of the music and the perfect partnership they had on the dance floor, she forgot to fight, and for a perfect moment there was nothing in the world but the new, beautiful feeling of his warm, soft lips on hers.

Then applause broke out and the world came back. Redmond let her go, caught her hand, and led her back, not to their table, but to the lounge setting, where their drinks had been set out for them on one of the coffee tables.

"That was nice," Lisa murmured, curling up in the corner of the sofa and fighting a sudden wave of sleepiness.

"You danced well. Pity I can't feed you a few drinks and a nice dinner before the competition. I thought dinner and a drink would make all the difference to you, make you relax a bit more."

All at once, Lisa was alert again. So that was what all this was about. Wine her and dine her and treat her nicely so that she'd perform for him.

"Jesus, Redmond Carrington, you are a manipulative shit at times."

Redmond stared. She supposed he'd never heard her use language like that before but then she'd never had occasion to.

"Lisa," he stammered, looking almost believably sorry, but she didn't want to hear what he had to say. She couldn't take any more of this up and down, hot and cold, fake/real relationship. She needed to get out.

"No, don't. You've said enough today. No wonder you wouldn't back me up with Tiffany. I'm nothing to you, am I, except a dancing robot? Well, I've had it with this. I'm going home. I'll see you at practice tomorrow. Don't call me before then."

She stood up. He caught at her but she wrenched her hand free of his grasp and fled.

Chapter 7

Outside, she realised she'd forgotten her coat but she wasn't about to go back. When she got to the underground station, she was in luck. A train was just about to leave in her direction, and she flung herself through the closing doors. There was no chance of Redmond following, even if he bothered coming after her, which she thought unlikely.

Once she'd got her breath back, she realised she felt ridiculous with her excessive makeup and the high heels she'd been dancing in. She wasn't overly made-up for a typical evening, but on Sunday night there weren't many clubbers out and about, and she was conscious of attracting more attention than she'd have liked. Still, everybody in the carriage looked amused rather than threatening, and for once she'd take a taxi at the other end rather than walking the last five minutes dressed like this. Apart from anything else, her shoes were going to start giving her blisters before long if she actually tried walking in them.

Sometimes you had to wait for a taxi at this time of night, but for once there were a couple waiting in line when she got off the train. She slipped into the front seat of the first one in line, and gave her destination. Belatedly, as the driver pulled out into the traffic, she wished she'd sat in the back. She didn't normally worry too much, but having put on a short skirt instead of her usual jeans after the filming, she felt uncomfortably exposed. She tried, without being too obvious about it, to keep her distance from where the taxi driver's hand rested on the gear lever.

He chatted the way taxi drivers did: had she been out with friends? Had a nice evening? Did she own her flat? How long had she lived there? Did her boyfriend live with her? She lied in answer to that last question—she always did. It was the only lie she permitted herself, but friends had convinced her it was a necessary one for a woman living on her own.

Finally the taxi driver turned into her road.

"This'll do fine," she said hastily, realising that she didn't want him pulling into the dimly lit courtyard outside her flat. At least here there were people passing, and cars, so if he tried anything she had a chance of getting help.

She didn't know why she'd suddenly got so suspicious—he hadn't said or done anything untoward, but something about the way he looked at her and his tone of voice gave her an uneasy feeling. When he showed no signs of slowing down, she realised her suspicions had been well founded.

"I'll take you to your door, miss," he said firmly, and Lisa prayed that was all he had in mind.

When the car pulled up outside her flat, she already had one hand on the door handle.

"How much is that?"

She reached for her handbag with her right hand, while tugging the door handle with her left. The door didn't budge.

"For you? How about a kiss? I won't tell if you don't."

She hadn't looked at him all the way back, but now she found herself noticing every detail of his unshaven chin, dark eyes, and unkempt black brows. She'd heard of rape and kidnap ordeals that began this way. His thick-knuckled fingers crept across her leg, making her skin crawl, and she wanted to slap him off, but what if he had a knife?

She tried to keep her voice level and polite, not wanting to risk upsetting him and making him still more unstable.

"Thanks, but if it's all the same to you, I'm happy to pay." She dug in her purse for a note.

"And if it's not the same to me?" he leered.

"Please, don't," she begged. Inspiration struck. "My boyfriend will be home any minute."

Mercifully, car headlights swung into the close behind her. Surely now he'd let her go.

"That'll be him now," she said desperately, as another taxi pulled up behind them and a tall figure stepped out.

The driver, unconvinced, lunged for her, his clumsy hand fumbling her breast. She heard a scream and realised it was her own voice. Then there was a bang on the window, and the driver started away abruptly.

The driver snatched the note from her hand and released the door with a click . Then Redmond was hauling her out onto the pavement. Before she'd had time to wonder how he came to be there, the taxi squealed off into the night and she was crying in Redmond's arms.

"Bastard! Are you OK? What happened? What did he do? Shall I call the police?"

Words tumbled across the top of Lisa's head but she couldn't seem to make her mouth respond. For the second time that evening, she was helpless, sobs shaking her shoulders and tears pouring down her face. Redmond held her tightly and this time, finally, she relaxed into his protective embrace. They stood like that for a long time. Redmond's taxi had gone and eventually they'd been still so long that the security light on the front of the building went out.

In the darkness, Lisa sobbed against Redmond's chest while he stood very still, one arm locked around her lower back and the other hand gently stroking and soothing her shoulders. His hand was warm, and suddenly she noticed the chill of the night against her bare skin and found herself shivering violently.

"Come on, let's get you inside." Redmond steered her towards the door. She let him take her handbag, fish out her keys, and lead her indoors.

Lisa watched him wrestling with the door of her flat.

"You have to pull it towards you as you turn the key," she explained. Somehow this piece of everyday information shook her back into her normal world and she looked around her as if for the first time since she emerged from the taxi.

Redmond gave the door a tug and it fell open. He held the door and gestured for Lisa to go inside. She paused in the doorway, looking up at him in bewilderment.

"What were you doing here?"

"You left..." He looked down at his empty hands and began to laugh.

"What's funny?"

"The joke's on me. You left your coat at the restaurant. I was going to give it back, but it's not here. I must have left it in the taxi. I'll ring them tomorrow and arrange to pick it up once I've got my car back. This evening wasn't very well planned. I shouldn't have driven to the restaurant and then had those cocktails."

Lisa was still a few steps behind, and not sure she'd understood him correctly. "You came all the way here by taxi to give me my coat?"

Lisa led him into the kitchen and put the kettle on out of force of habit. It was usually the first thing she did when she came in.

"Well, and to make sure you were OK. You did seem to be in a bit of a state tonight, if you don't mind my saying so, and I wanted to be sure you got home all right. Turns out it's a good thing I did."

Lisa mechanically put teabags and milk in two mugs before remembering that Redmond took his tea black.

"Sorry. I'm not quite with it." She gave a rueful smile.

"I should be doing that. Why don't you sit down? Or phone the police if you feel up to it."

"What's the point? So I tell them a taxi driver tried to kiss me, didn't threaten me or hurt me, and drove off when you banged on the window. What are they going to do about it?"

"Nothing, probably, but at least they'll have the information on file to use against him if he tries it on someone else."

"I suppose so." Lisa perched on a stool and watched numbly

as Redmond took over the tea making. "I don't have the car registration anyway. And I can't remember what the guy looked like, except he had black hair and big hands."

She shuddered, remembering the feel of his thick fingers creeping across her skin.

Redmond caught the movement and was at her side in a moment, pressing a mug of tea into her hands and slipping an arm around her shoulders.

She sipped the hot, sweet drink gratefully.

"Are you still cold?" Redmond asked. "Shall I find you a jumper?"

Truthfully, she was warm enough with his arm around her, but it wasn't wise to sit like this any longer than she had to. She waved her arm towards the jumper hanging over the back of a chair, and Redmond immediately dropped it into her hand.

"Is there anything else I can do?" Redmond asked earnestly.

She gave him her tea to hold while she put the jumper on and thought about what she wanted done.

She supposed he was right about calling the police.

"Find the number for the police station?" she suggested.

Watching as he found and dialed the number, she noticed again how much at home he looked here. She thought he must have a lot of experience of settling into other women's homes.

Just because he'd turned up at the right moment tonight, she mustn't let herself be fooled into thinking she mattered to him, at least as anything more than a friend and dancing partner. If she'd been raped or murdered on the way home, or fallen down a flight of stairs at the underground, she'd not have been much use to him in the competition. That was why he was here.

Redmond held out the phone to her and she took it just as someone at the other end picked up.

"I'd like to report an incident," she said, wondering just which cheesy cop show she'd picked up that phrase from. Actually, she wouldn't like to report the incident. She'd like it if it had never happened.

She went through the police officer's questions as if completing an exam paper. Many of them she couldn't answer, and she kept wondering if the answers would come to her when she woke in the middle of the night.

When she'd answered everything she could, Redmond gestured to be passed the phone. She handed it over, wondering what he was going to add.

"I might be able to fill in some more details, if that would be helpful," he suggested politely.

Evidently the police officer agreed, because he then described in detail the taxi that had dropped Lisa off, including the registration, colour, and a scratch on the rear wing. The driver was apparently about six one—as best as Redmond could judge with him sitting down—dark skinned and haired, unshaven (Lisa remembered that but had forgotten to say it), and had a scar on the back of one arm.

As Redmond hung up, Lisa looked at him in astonishment.

"Did you used to be in the CIA or something?"

Redmond grinned. "Those that ask no questions..." he said, tapping the side of his nose in what she was sure he knew was an absolutely infuriating way.

"Redmond," she said, warningly. She was in no mood for jokes.

He sobered instantly. "No, but I did work as a security guard for a while in Florida."

She nodded. That made sense. More sense than him being a secret CIA agent. She didn't think they took on foreign nationals anyway.

"More tea?" Redmond asked, noticing her empty mug.

"I'll do it," Lisa said, standing up and slipping in her silly shoes on the smooth kitchen floor. She kicked her shoes off impatiently and padded over to the kettle.

"You sit down," Redmond said, in a tone that permitted no argument. "You've had a shock. This is one time you really can't object to being looked after."

"Why would I object?"

Redmond sighed heavily, as if she was an exasperating toddler asking silly questions. "You know," he said.

"No, I don't know. I wouldn't have asked if I knew."

"You mean you haven't noticed you have this whole independence thing going? Like, I'll pay for that, I'll get that, I'll do that, no don't hold the door for me…"

Lisa gave an embarrassed laugh as the truth of what he'd said hit home.

She did hate having things done for her. Unlike the girls at work, she'd always had to do things for herself, and she was proud of it. She didn't want anything compromising her independence—especially not Redmond, with his forceful personality, his newfound wealth, and his easy, assured way of taking charge of any situation. In fact, she thought guiltily, once she'd got over the initial shock of the taxi incident, she'd started to think she could have handled things herself, and had almost resented him for turning up and taking away her chance to prove her independence.

She threw up her hands. "OK, I admit it. You're right. So you're in charge. What do I do now?"

"Go and sit down somewhere comfortable while I make some more tea. Relax. Put some nice music on or something."

Lisa stuck some Bach in the CD player and stretched out on the sofa.

She must have drifted off because all of a sudden she felt a hand brush her leg, and she yelped and flinched away. Opening her eyes, she found Redmond settling a blanket over her.

"Sorry, I didn't mean to make you jump. I didn't want you getting cold. You've had a shock."

"So you keep saying," Lisa snapped. "I didn't need reminding."

Then she felt guilty for snapping.

"Sorry," she mumbled. "I don't mean to bite your head off. You did give me a scare. I still feel… I don't know…" She groped for the word. "Nasty. Grubby. When you touched me, it reminded me of him touching me. Yuk!"

Redmond looked at her with deep concern.

"It's OK," she reassured him. "It's nothing, really. I just wasn't thinking straight. I was half asleep. What happened to that tea?"

Redmond waved a hand towards the coffee table, where the mug was steaming away. "Shall I pass it?"

Lisa was just about to snap, "I can get it, I'm not an invalid," when she remembered his earlier comment about her stubborn independence. Well, why not take advantage of having a willing slave for the evening?

"Please."

She stretched out a hand, and this time when his fingers brushed hers, she forced herself not to flinch. It wasn't as hard as she'd feared. Apparently, awake, her body knew the difference between Redmond and a lecherous taxi driver.

She tucked her feet up underneath her on the couch. "Sorry," she apologised.

"What for?"

"Not leaving you anywhere to sit."

"I'm fine here."

Lisa laughed. He'd obviously taken her reaction to heart and was now keeping his distance.

"It's OK. I don't bite and now I'm awake I don't expect you to either. Come and sit here."

He did so.

"Thanks."

"For?"

"Looking after me. The tea. Turning up."

"No problem. I'm glad I'm here."

"So am I."

Redmond looked stunned.

"What's so surprising about that?" she demanded.

"You've been acting so stroppy since I came back, I thought you hated me."

"So why did you think I was dancing with you?"

"Because Elaine and Mark twisted your arm, of course. They knew I wanted to dance with you, and the publicity would do the studio good."

Redmond looked as if he was about to add something, but thought better of it. Lisa almost asked what, but her mind had snagged on one part of his remark and stuck there.

"Whoa, hang on. You really wanted to dance with me?"

"Of course."

"Not of course," Lisa echoed back. "Obviously I wanted to dance with you—you're miles better than any of the guys here—but I didn't think you'd be bothered after all the good partners you must have had in America."

"Yes, America's so full of unique, lovely girls, that's why I came back to find you."

"You came back..." Lisa's mouth refused to even shape the words. It was all too bizarre. "Elaine said you came back on business."

"Personal business, I think was the phrase she used."

Lisa thought back to her conversation with Elaine and nodded slowly. Perhaps it had been. "Something equally vague, anyway," Lisa conceded. "What on earth did she mean by it?"

"She didn't know. I wasn't going to say anything until I saw how the land lay. I'd been hearing rumours about you and Jerry, and I knew I wasn't exactly in your good books after scarpering so suddenly. So this competition looked like the ideal way to test the water."

"Me and Jerry?" The whole conversation was so odd, Lisa didn't know what to latch onto first, but out of it all that was perhaps the thing that surprised her most. Sure, she and Jerry didn't exactly fight the rumours—it kept guys off her back and his parents off his—but how in the world had that got back to Redmond?

Redmond nodded, grinning. "Of course, as soon as I saw him it was obvious he's ragingly gay. That was when I started to think I might be in with a chance."

"And what do you think now?" Lisa was still struggling to keep up with the workings of his mind.

"I don't know. What should I think?"

Lisa shook her head, bemused. She didn't know what to say. In fact, she wasn't even sure what he was asking.

"I don't know," she mirrored. "I'm confused."

"You and me both, babe," Redmond drawled in an exaggerated American accent. "Are you going to tell me what was up with you tonight? You looked happy enough to come out with me after filming, and then we got to the restaurant and suddenly you started on me as if I'd committed some mortal sin. And for what? Keeping you out of trouble in the studio and ordering some drinks. So I don't want to get caught up in fighting with that overgrown toddler, and I wanted to impress you at the restaurant. Is that so bad?"

Lisa frowned. She couldn't explain that what made it so difficult was the ease with which he took control.

"Jesus, girl," Redmond went on impassionedly, losing the last trace of Americanism, "you don't half make it difficult for me. I've put a good job in America on hold to come back and partner you, and I've turned up to every practice and danced my heart out. I've done my damndest not to pressure you into anything even though you're even more stunning now than when I left, and that's saying something. And I turned up here tonight to make sure you were OK even after your performance in the restaurant. So, please, if I've done something wrong, could you at least tell me what it is? Because the way I see it, I've done everything possible to convince you I care about you. Am I wrong?"

Lisa stared. He sounded as if he meant it.

"You care? That's not how it looked from this end when you walked off into the sunset and vanished for years on end. Do you have any idea how much that hurt? And then when I suggested that we could give it a go, being together, you came back with some feeble put-down about not rushing into anything. So excuse me if I find it a little hard to take you seriously when you waltz back into my life with a cute smile and some flattering words and expect me to fall at your feet just so you can trample on me again."

"So I made a mistake. I'm here now, saying I'm sorry and I won't do it again. What can I do to persuade you? Or are you determined to keep punishing me for one mistake for the rest of our lives?"

Suddenly Lisa didn't know what to say or where to look. In a few breaths they'd gone from arguing over his reaction to Tiffany's antics to talking about the rest of their lives. She seemed to have been longing for this moment forever, and yet it was so utterly unlike how she'd imagined it… if she'd ever dared to imagine it at all. Come to think of it, she wasn't sure she had. What would she have put her money on? Romantic declarations? Redmond wasn't the wordy type. She'd imagined he'd do something to show his feelings, but then, hadn't he already done that, day after day, going out of his way to make sure she was taken care of, even following her home after she'd stormed out on him?

She shook her head wonderingly.

It had been there all along, and she'd just never seen it.

Chapter 8

"Lisa?" Redmond leaned towards her with an enquiring look.

She stared back, refusing to give anything away too easily. For all these years, she'd been convinced she meant nothing to him, and now he turned around and told her that the exact opposite was true. OK, so it was true he was treating her differently. He was kinder, gentler and more caring, but at the end of the day he had to be the same old Redmond. He might be asking her to reinterpret the past, but he still wasn't making any promises. Not that she'd ask him to. Not yet, anyway. Better to take things a step at a time.

"OK, say I'm persuaded." She let herself smile at him, showing a hint of the excitement that was bubbling up at the thought that he might really mean it. "What happens now?"

"Well, I would say we go out and shout it from the rooftops, but we've already told everyone anyway. Trust us to do everything backwards."

Redmond laughed his joyous, infectious laugh and threw an affectionate arm around her shoulders. Lisa leaned into his embrace, sharing in the laughter. She'd expected the world suddenly to feel different, but if anything things seemed to feel more normal than they had for some time. The easy camaraderie she'd shared with Redmond before he left was back, and it felt perfectly natural to snuggle closer into his chest and rest her hand on his warm, firm thigh.

The only problem was, it felt so good she couldn't quite believe it was happening.

"Is this for real?" The words had slipped out before she'd realised she'd spoken.

"Real?" Redmond pulled back until he could look her in the eye again. "Does this feel real to you?"

Once again, his lips were on hers, but this time he held nothing back. His warm tongue teased her mouth into opening for him, tasting his warmth and the slight tang of alcohol on his breath. It felt real, and wonderful. Lisa let herself feel that, yes, it was real. His warm hands on her shoulders. His lips on hers. It was all so real, so perfect, that she hardly dared to let herself breathe, in case she spoiled the moment. Finally he pulled back, just far enough to let her see the desire in his blue eyes. And she believed in that. But, after all this time, how could she be certain it was enough?

"Redmond?" When her breath returned, she forced herself to ask, one final time. "Are you sure this isn't just because of the show?"

"Lisa, look at me." The stern schoolteacher voice was at odds with the way he sprawled casually on the sofa, keeping his arm around her. His face was serious, but there was just the tiniest hint of amusement in his voice as he continued. "I've loved you more or less from the moment I saw you. I know I haven't always picked the best way of showing it, but believe me, everything I've done, no matter how stupid, was always done with the best intention of making you happy. I only took the job in America because I knew there was no way I'd have made that kind of money over here, with the experience I had at the time. I always meant to come back, it just took me a bit longer than I intended, and that was a mistake, but I'm doing my best to make up for it. If there's anything more I can do to make you happy, you have only to say."

"Anything?" Lisa said in a small voice, wondering if she dared ask the one thing that would make a difference. She didn't want him to go back to America. Not now. Not next week. Not next year. Not ever. At that moment, if she could have kept him beside her forever, with his strong arm around her shoulders, she would have done it.

But could she do that to him? He had a life there. She'd followed the gossip long enough to know how successful he was—and let's face it, he had to be successful to be enough of a talking point for news of his life to travel halfway round the world to her.

No, she couldn't ask him to leave it all for her. If he did so, it had to be his own choice. Perhaps she could make him want to stay, but that was something that would come in time. For now, it was enough to have him here, making her feel wanted and cared for in a way that no one else had.

Which gave her an idea. His comment seemed to demand an answer, but she wasn't quite ready to give a serious one. She didn't want to know how far his new devotion extended. But she did want something: one perfect evening being protected and loved. Starting with erasing all memory of the horrible start to the evening, which had turned out to be such a blessing in disguise.

"There's one thing you can do. Run me a bath. With lots of bubbles."

He looked at her quizzically. "Are you sure? You wouldn't rather ask for a diamond ring or a limousine?"

"I don't wear jewellery and there's not enough parking space around here for limos. I just want to relax, give my ankle a soak, and get the feel of those horrible grubby hands off me."

"Of course."

Redmond sprang to attention and was gone.

Her shoulders felt cold and bare where his arm had been. For a moment she regretted saying anything that made him move, even for a minute or two. She didn't want to end the perfect moment in case something spoiled it. What if she, or he, had a chance to think and realised they'd made a mistake? What if they spoiled their friendship? Although she had to admit that at the moment it didn't feel as if that would be a consequence of their move from friends to... what?

Lisa was still pondering the thorny question when he returned. Could she class Redmond as her boyfriend? Despite her insistence to Tim and everyone else on the show that Red was her boyfriend, she found the term slightly absurd. There was nothing at all of "boy" about Redmond's rugged physique, much less his formidable intellect and personality? Should it be her lover? Considering they'd had more physical contact in some of their dances than they had that evening, the term didn't seem any more appropriate.

"Madam's bath awaits," Redmond interrupted her thoughts, striking a casual but effective pose in the doorway as he performed his impression of an obsequious servant.

"Stop it," Lisa instructed him, only half seriously. "You'll make me feel guilty. You did ask."

"I know. I told you—anything for you. Are you sure that's all I can do? You wouldn't like me to come and undress you too?"

Lisa found her heart beating faster at the thought. She wasn't used to the new, openly flirtatious Redmond, and she didn't know how to respond.

Redmond sensed her discomfort and immediately backtracked. "Joke, sweetheart. I know the last thing you want at the moment is any man's grubby mitts on you. I'll stay out of your way, but shout if you need anything."

"Thank you," Lisa said, and fled for the bathroom before she could change her mind. She knew he was doing the right thing. They'd waited this long. They could wait a little longer, until her mind was free of unpleasant thoughts about the evening's experiences.

Still, it was strange, undressing in the privacy of her own home, yet knowing that just a thin wall separated her from Redmond. She heard the distinctive creak of the sofa's old springs as he settled down, then a muted mumbling of voices indicated that he had turned on the television. She was grateful for that—she'd felt self-conscious about him sitting there listening to her moving about.

Now she was free to lie back and swoosh the water gently around her, watching miniature tides moving the bubbles up and down.

She assessed her body critically. With all the dancing, and the haste causing her to skip meals, she was slimmer than she'd ever been. Mostly, she liked that, although she was also perhaps a shade flatter-chested than she had been, and that she didn't like. Looking down at her small, neat breasts, she found herself assailed again by the memory of the taxi driver's dark, hungry hands. She shuddered and ran her own hands across her skin, willing herself to remember how a touch could be pleasant instead of intrusive.

She tried to imagine Redmond's hands on her bare skin. How would she feel if he touched her now? Her mind was still uncertain, but her body responded, enjoying the imagined caresses, the desire she read in his eyes. She'd seen it before, she realised now, in odd moments on the dance floor, when she appeared in front of him in a particularly enticing outfit, or in their conspiratorial moments when she leaned in to whisper some cheeky remark not intended for the rest of the world. She'd just never seen it for what it was, and now that she did, the world suddenly seemed like an entirely different place.

She'd never really wanted anyone else, but somehow she'd assumed that her lack of interest in all the men who passed through the studio meant that she was somehow above that kind of thing. Now she realised how wrong she'd been. Her body was capable of a level of desire she'd never even imagined, and the strange new feeling shook her, leaving her feeling weak and uncertain. She wanted Redmond's hands on her skin, his lips on hers, his body against her, and yet the thought frightened her. She knew a word from her would bring him running, yet her lips remained firmly closed.

It was just too much, too soon for her to adjust to. This new turn of events had forced her to reassess everything she'd thought she'd known. Facts and interpretations shuffled themselves into new arrangements, memories changed their hue viewed through a different understanding of the world. She suspected that what she really wanted to wash off was not the taxi driver's grubbiness, but the confusion and uncertainty that surrounded her thinking about Redmond, their past, and their future.

It had seemed so much simpler with his arms around her.

With that thought, she lost interest in languishing in the now-tepid water. She pulled the plug out, stood up, and wrapped herself in the towel that Redmond had left warming on the radiator for her.

As she walked to her bedroom, she had a sudden vision of running into him in the hall. Towels weren't the most reliable covering in the world, and she could imagine it slipping into a damp heap on the floor and leaving her exposed to his gaze. And his touch.

She could imagine how he'd crush her in his arms, how his hands would roam freely over her body in the way that their suggestive dance routines had implied for so long. Her body responded to the sensations as if they were real, and suddenly she was tired of being shy and restrained. She pulled her most seductive negligee from the dresser drawer, slipped it on, and returned to the lounge before her nerve could desert her.

The television was on, but Redmond was stretched out on the sofa with his eyes closed.

She flicked the television off.

"I was watching that."

"Really? I thought you were asleep."

"I woke up."

"Oh, really? I thought maybe you were talking in your sleep. It's not all that easy to tell."

Just two steps brought him to her side, where he caught her hands and pinned them neatly in front of her.

"I think you meant to say something different. Am I right?" His threatening tone was defused by the suppressed laughter shaking his body.

"I don't think so. I thought I made myself quite clear."

"Really? How unfortunate." She wasn't sure quite how he managed it, but suddenly she was sprawling back on the sofa, with Redmond kneeling over her, urging, "Submit!"

"Never!" she insisted, twisting one wrist free from his grip. That proved to be a mistake, as far as winning the fight went, because it enabled him to pin the free hand above her head so that she was stretched out helplessly beneath him. Not that she minded. She quite enjoyed lying back and looking up at his broad shoulders and smiling face. Her wrist, encircled in his strong grasp, felt slim and fragile.

"Ha ha," Redmond gave a mock maniacal cackle. "Now you are in my power."

Lisa laughed. "I think you need to practise the evil laugh a bit more," she remarked casually.

Redmond's response was to stretch her arm a little further above her head, while pinning her legs down with one of his own.

"Ve haff vays of mekking you talk," he intoned.

Lisa stubbornly closed her mouth.

Redmond released one hand and ran a finger gently around her lips.

She briefly considered using her free hand to good effect by pinching, tickling, or otherwise annoying him, but as he lowered his lips to hers, she forgot even to pretend to fight. His kiss was gentle but insistent. In spite of themselves, her lips parted to welcome him.

Lisa's free hand moved of its own accord, twining itself in Redmond's soft hair and drawing him closer against her. Through her thin nightgown, she was painfully aware of his firm body against her, and she thought she could feel the hard warmth of his arousal against her stomach.

The kiss seemed to last forever, but all too soon Redmond pulled away for breath. Lisa took the opportunity to free her other hand and tug hungrily at Redmond's shirt, tucking her hand inside and running it over all she could reach of his muscular back and sharp shoulder blades. With her hand on his back, she was able to pull him closer against her, and he responded to her touch, first kissing her lips and then drawing back to drop small, gentle kisses on her cheeks, neck, and breasts.

"That's nice," she murmured.

Redmond laughed and hauled himself up until his head was right next to her ear, before whispering a response.

"I told you I'd make you talk."

"You…" Lisa spluttered.

"Shh." Redmond trailed kisses from her earlobe down her cheek to her lips, where he lingered sensuously.

Lisa forgot about protesting. Everything felt so good. Her whole body seemed to be a million times more aware than usual. Every inch of skin and every nerve ending seemed to crackle with life. Her fingers took in Redmond's smooth, firm skin and the softness of the hair at the nape of his neck, while her mouth pressed him for ever more insistent kisses.

Redmond propped himself on one elbow and pulled away for a moment.

Lisa reached upwards, intent on keeping her lips in contact with his, teasing out of him a few more tender kisses.

Redmond put a hand on her shoulder, restraining her. She struggled for a moment, but he turned the pressure into a gentle stroking, and she relaxed under his soothing touch. He knelt beside her, running both hands over her shoulders and upper arms, playing around the straps of her nightgown and occasionally letting his fingers stray under the light silk to play around the curves of her breasts.

"Mmm." Lisa heard small, quiet sounds of enjoyment, and realised that they were her own.

"Bedtime?" Redmond asked, finally letting one hand rest for a moment cupping her breast. She arched upwards, moulding her body against him.

"Yes." Lisa's voice had become husky, hungry, a sensuous feminine sound she'd never known herself capable of.

Redmond swept her into his arms and carried her to her bed, then stepped away from her. In the dim light that filtered through the curtains, she could just about make out his body moving as he undressed.

"Are you sleepy?" he murmured, moving closer to her and slipping one arm around her waist.

She, in return, put a hand out and encountered his bare chest, lean and muscular. She found her fingertips caressing him as she paused to consider her answer, and he in turn gave a low, contented sigh.

"A little," she said, not entirely truthfully. She was a lot sleepy, but she didn't want the evening to end just yet.

She pressed closer against him and let her hand slide across his chest and down his back to his waist, where the smoothness of skin gave way to the softness of brushed cotton. Perversely, despite her nervousness, she found herself wishing she'd found only bare skin. She had a sudden urge to pull away the inconvenient barrier of clothing between them, but didn't quite dare, so she contented herself with running her hands lightly over his back, chest and legs, tantalising both him and herself by occasionally straying across the front of his shorts, letting him know that she could feel his arousal.

He responded by slipping the straps of her nightgown off her shoulders and letting his fingers play gently across her face, neck, and bare breasts. As he teased her nipples into firmness, her breath came in short gasps. She tried to breathe naturally, but each time his fingers found a sensitive spot, she would find herself taking a sharp, excited breath.

Her body, normally so controlled, took on a life of its own. Her breathing was ragged; she found her voice reacting of its own accord, gasping with pleasure, whimpering with desire, and occasionally gasping his name as if it were a demand, or whispering it like a sensuous caress. Her body arched itself in pleasure again and again at his touch.

"Sure you're not sleepy?" he teased, pulling her into a crushing embrace. Every inch of her body felt warm and alive, and she could feel, too, how much he wanted her.

She shook her head vigorously and then buried her face in his neck, kissing randomly wherever her lips landed.

Unbidden, her mouth, finding itself next to his ear, whispered gently, nervously, but firmly, "I want you."

Instantly, embarrassed, she buried her face back against his shoulder. She couldn't believe she'd said that.

"I want you too." Redmond's voice was throaty, deep, and low and desperately sexy. Encouraged, Lisa ran her hands more firmly over his body, massaging his back and buttocks, and finally sliding her fingers under the waist of his underwear.

"Lee," he murmured, and something about his tone made her pause.

She pulled back, letting her hands rest where they were on his lean hips, enjoying the feel of his skin against hers. As best she could in the low light, she looked into his eyes. His expression was serious.

"Mmm?" What was the matter? Surely she couldn't have mistaken his feelings. His body told her otherwise, and he'd even said he wanted her too. She frowned, baffled.

"Let's just go to sleep, huh?"

Now she was really bemused. Sleep was the last thing on her mind and, she would have said until a moment earlier, on his too. Her body ached with desire. No way would she sleep until she at least understood what was behind this sudden change.

"Why?" She racked her brains for an explanation. "Did I do something wrong?"

Redmond chuckled dryly and dropped a kiss on her forehead. "Of course not. I just don't think this is the right time."

His opposition drove her to a new level of boldness.

"It feels like a good time to me," she argued, a firm pressure of her hand making sure her meaning was not mistaken.

A short intake of breath on his part told her that he was not uninterested. So what was going on?

"Oh, Lee." Once again he used his old nickname for her, which nobody else seemed to have adopted. In some strange way it restored her faith in their relationship. Whatever was happening now, they'd get through it. She gave him what she hoped was a reassuring smile, and he continued slowly, "It's been a strange evening. You've had a lot to drink and a big shock and I don't want to take advantage of the fact that everything feels different today. If you still feel the same way when things are back to normal, I won't need asking twice."

"Really?" If it hadn't been so tragic, Lisa would have laughed at the forlorn hopelessness of her tone of voice. She wanted him now—not tomorrow or next week—but how was she ever going to convince him of that, if he didn't think she was in a fit state to make the decision?

"Yes, really," he said, a touch impatiently, she thought. "Now will you go to sleep?"

"I'm not tired," she said petulantly, but a huge yawn gave her away.

Suddenly they were both laughing and all the tension drained away.

"Come on," Redmond said, in the friendly coaxing manner she remembered so well. "Give me a hug and then let's get some sleep."

Intentionally or otherwise, he kept his distance slightly, so that the hug was friendly rather than sexual. Lisa was already beginning to get over her annoyance at the situation. There would be plenty more nights. To know Redmond cared for her after all, and to have him sleeping beside her, was more than enough for one day.

She settled down beside him, listening to the unaccustomed sound of slow breathing in her ear. It was so peaceful.

A smile spread across Lisa's face, and then she drifted into sleep.

Chapter 9

It seemed only a moment later that Lisa was roused by a shrill, unfamiliar ringing, which told her immediately that something had changed. She always woke to a CD of gentle music to ease her into the day. This wasn't her alarm, nor was it the familiar ring tone of her phone.

She looked around, puzzled, and lit on Redmond's face beside her. Recollection dawned.

She'd slept soundly, more tired than she'd realised from her eventful day. Judging by the light streaming through the curtains, she'd also slept for longer than she'd expected.

Beside her, Redmond pushed back the covers and stumbled sleepily towards the heap of clothes on the floor from which the noise was emanating. It must be his mobile—that was why the tone was unfamiliar to her. She lay back and watched through half-closed eyes as Redmond, dressed only in a brief pair of shorts, leaned over and rummaged for his phone. The whole situation felt slightly unreal. She could hardly remember the last time she'd had a guy in her flat, never mind in her bedroom, and now here she was lying in bed watching him wandering around in his underwear as casually as if he'd woken in his own home.

Redmond retrieved the phone and snapped out a greeting, settling himself on the edge of the bed with his long limbs tucked up underneath him.

"Sorry," he mouthed over his shoulder at Lisa, who gave a wry grin.

Actually, she wasn't sorry she'd been woken. It must be time she got up anyway, although the alarm hadn't gone off so it couldn't be too late. And if they'd stayed asleep, she wouldn't have been able to admire Redmond's bare, muscular body as he spoke.

"No, not at all," he said after a brief silence. "We were just getting up anyway." He flashed Lisa a grin and shifted back across the bed so that he was sitting near enough to play with her hair as he talked.

"Tonight? Yes, I should think so. I'll check. Hang on."

Redmond put his phone on mute.

"What?" Lisa asked sleepily.

"Tim wants the crew to come and film our practice tonight."

Lisa was pleased now that she'd tried dancing in the restaurant. At least she knew her ankle would hold out. She wouldn't have wanted to be worrying about it all day, but she also wouldn't like to turn down the camera crew. She knew the competition was as much a popularity contest as a test of their dancing skills.

"Is that OK?" Redmond continued.

She nodded, and Redmond leaned down to plant a kiss on her lips before returning to the phone call.

"No problem," he told Tim, and made a few more arrangements before ringing off.

"We're on!" Redmond flung his phone somewhere in the heap of covers and folded Lisa into his arms. "They love us. I knew they would. Now we just need to win!"

"Funny he phoned so early, though," Lisa remarked.

Redmond looked down at her, amused. "Why, how early do you think it is?"

"Well, my alarm hasn't gone off, so it must be before…" Lisa trailed off as it dawned on her what was wrong with that assumption. Normally she set the alarm on her way to bed, but last night her mind had been elsewhere. "Oh hell!" Worse words had crossed her mind but she didn't want to sound too unladylike. "What time is it?"

"Are you sure you want to know?"

"Stop teasing me!"

"Why? It's so much fun." But when she reached for Redmond's watch from the bedside table, he didn't try to stop her.

Ten fifteen.

"Shit!" This time Lisa didn't even try to restrain herself.

"Is it that bad?"

"Yes!" She'd just remembered Gary and his long overdue designs. And her boss was in the office today, so if Gary had called, he'd be the first to know. And he was already edgy about her continually leaving "early"—technically on time, but since when had a boss ever taken any notice of an insignificant matter like a contract—for dancing.

"So ring in sick."

"Half way through the morning? Unless you're at death's door, you ring before nine."

"So what's your excuse?"

"I don't know. I'll think of something on the way."

But everything she thought of was hopelessly lame, so it was a relief when her colleague greeted her loudly with, "How did it go? I told Alan about your doctor's appointment—he said to remind you to put them in your calendar in future."

"Sorry, I thought I had," Lisa played along, with a huge sigh of relief. "It wasn't too bad but they were running a bit late. I'll stay over lunch to make it up."

Afternoon arrived quickly, and Lisa soon had to hurry off for filming. There was only time to grab a quick sandwich, which she ate on the bus. Then she hurried breathlessly into the studio, only to discover that Redmond wasn't there. She took a deep breath and sat down to put on her dance shoes.

Redmond came in as she was adjusting the buckle, and her resolution to stay calm flew out the door as he entered.

"Where were you?" she snapped.

"Sorry. I had to make a call. Didn't Elaine tell you? I asked her to."

Lisa had wanted to know who he was calling and why, but she supposed he was entitled to make a phone call without her biting his head off. She didn't want the first thing the cameras recorded to be a lovers' tiff. If that was what it was. She was still a little uncertain about their relationship, quite prepared to find that it had been a moment's madness born of the strangeness of the previous night. But even if it was, they had at least to pretend to continue the madness, so she reached up and kissed him hello.

"Never mind." She smiled through gritted teeth. "You're here now."

"So let's dance," Redmond said cheerfully, linking his arm through hers and leading her to the end of the dance floor nearest the cameras.

He gave a small nod to Elaine and music filled the room. Lisa wondered if she'd caught a shred of mischief in Redmond's smile, but the hint had not prepared her for the torture that followed. For a start, it was a faster jive than she was used to, and then Redmond kept adapting their old routine to fit the unfamiliar song, so that she couldn't even rely on knowing what came next to help her keep the pace up. Even though she'd been practising jive day after day, for hours on end, for most of her adult life, she was still panting when it came to the end of the first track.

It was worth it, though, for the spontaneous ripple of applause that ran through the studio as they came to a halt. Only then did Lisa realise that most of the other couples had stopped dancing partway through to watch them. She stared around the room, eyes wide with surprise and mouth half-open, catching at breath.

"Not too hard for you?" Redmond said solicitously, slipping a protective arm around her shoulders in a way that Lisa found amusing, given that he was the one who had practically tried to dance her into the ground. Well, she wasn't going to be beaten.

She took a deep breath to make sure she could get the words out without panting, and said sweetly, "Oh, was that meant to be difficult? I didn't realise."

Redmond grinned. "I didn't think it was anything you couldn't handle, but it was mildly tricky, yes."

That floored her. She wanted to say that it was a bit more than "mildly tricky" but her mock innocence meant that she had to go along with the pretence that she hadn't seen it as anything difficult. Which meant that the next go round would only get harder. She suspected Redmond was testing her limits, but she supposed that was OK. Better do it now, even with the TV crew watching, than in the competition next Saturday.

The TV crew seemed happy enough, anyway. Over the course of the evening they fiddled around with the lighting a bit and occasionally asked for a few steps to be repeated, but by and large everyone soon got used to working around them. In fact, by the time Tim came over to ask if he could speak to Lisa, she was almost surprised to see him.

"Why me?" she asked, bewildered. Redmond was so much the more articulate of the two.

"No reason," Tim said. "I'll get both of you separately anyway. I just thought I'd ask you first. Maybe because you're prettiest."

"Good reason." Redmond nodded approvingly, looking Lisa slowly up and down in a way that evoked the blush she'd managed to avoid when Tim first made his comment.

Suddenly the whole competition seemed like an inconvenient interruption to the real business of being with Redmond. Which was funny, considering the competition was the only reason she was even speaking to him at all. She remembered how much she'd wanted not even to see him when he returned, but already that feeling was unimaginable. Why would she ever want to be anywhere but wherever he was?

But for now Tim was ushering her into Elaine's office.

"No Phillipa today?" Lisa enquired.

"No. I'm co-presenting with Phillipa. Mostly she'll be hosting you in the studio, and I'll be taking the cameras out and about."

"Fair enough." Although Tim annoyed her, it was something of a relief to know she wouldn't spend the evening watching Red chatting easily away with the stunning blonde presenter.

"So, tell me about how you and Redmond met," Tim requested, training the camera on her face. She didn't know where to look. She vaguely remembered hearing that you shouldn't look directly at the camera, but found that when she tried not to, she ended up conversing with the man's ear. Which was also somewhat disconcerting. Finally she gave up and recounted the story directly to the big black lens.

She kept thinking of things she'd missed, but didn't want to jump around too much, so most of them just got left out. Maybe if she got a chance she'd find a way to slip them in later. Anyway, the most important thing was not to incriminate herself about the fact that she and Redmond hadn't been a couple when it all began. Suddenly she had free rein to relax and talk freely about all the times she'd longed to be more than just dance partners, but the habit of biting her tongue was so ingrained that it was hard to stop herself choking back her more affectionate remarks.

How ironic, she thought, describing in a little less detail than she could have done how she'd felt when Redmond left for America, that now she had permission—and reason—to talk as freely as she liked, she wasn't enjoying doing it. Apart from anything else, Lisa wasn't the sort of girl who wore her heart on her sleeve. She kept her private life to herself. If she hadn't, word might eventually have got back to Redmond about her feelings for him, and maybe everything could have been different. Or not.

Tim was asking her if she regretted not getting together with Red sooner, and she found it surprisingly hard to answer the question. The truth was she simply couldn't imagine things happening any way other than how they had, so that was what she said. At least, she hoped that was what she'd said... when Tim finally lowered the camera and gave her a nod and a smile, she found she couldn't exactly remember what had come out of her mouth.

She said as much to Redmond when she got outside and he asked her what they'd spoken about.

"I don't know what I said. I really don't!" she exclaimed, then realised she sounded hysterical, and paused to take a deep breath. "He asked me questions and I was so nervous I just kept saying the first thing that came into my head and it probably made no sense at all."

"I expect it makes more sense than you think," he reassured her. "You're usually pretty coherent."

"Yes, but I usually don't have a bloody great camera staring me in the face and the prospect of half the country listening to my answer. It's unnerving, I can tell you. You wait until you're in there."

As if on cue, Tim came over to call Redmond in.

Lisa had expected to find a million ways she could have done better and things she should have said, but the truth was that her mind was blank even of improvements or regrets. The nerves seemed to have erased her brain completely, and all she could do was stare at the door and wait for Redmond to emerge, which he did ten minutes later, smiling broadly.

"We're done for the evening," he said. "Dinnertime?"

"I guess so." Lisa was suddenly uncomfortably conscious that they hadn't discussed where their relationship was going or what they expected from each other. She liked having him around, but would she want him staying every night after dancing? It would be a big change. And how would she ever get any work done? She supposed it was something they could talk about later, although she knew from other female friends that conversations like that didn't come easily to men anyway, so maybe she should just wait and see what happened.

Chapter 10

What happened was that Redmond strolled with her to the bus stop, so it seemed to make sense to invite him back for dinner, although she still hadn't been shopping so she wasn't sure what there would be to eat.

"Never mind." Redmond grinned. "You look good enough to eat in that dress."

"I don't think I'm edible," Lisa laughed, but suddenly she was uncomfortably conscious of how inappropriately she was dressed. She didn't want a repeat of the previous night's unpleasant experience. Still, this time Redmond was with her. She linked her hand into his and he shifted closer to her as if aware of her discomfort.

Redmond pulled her hand to his lips and nibbled experimentally on her fingertip. "Tastes good to me," was his verdict.

"Feels good, too." Lisa was surprised to find that the gentle pressure of his teeth tantalised, rather than irritated her.

Mind you, after last night, she suspected that just about anything would tantalise her. She realised now that, apart from the oversleeping incident, the other reason she'd spent so much of the day on edge was frustration at the way the previous night had turned out. She wanted Redmond so much, and she hoped that he'd meant what he said about not asking twice if she was still interested today. The paranoid part of her mind that refused to believe things could possibly be this good was still searching for reasons why he might have changed his mind over the course of the day.

Well, she'd find out soon enough. Their stop arrived, and Redmond kept hold of Lisa's hand as they got off the bus and walked up to the flat.

At the door, Lisa had already extricated her hand and rummaged in her bag for her keys before she remembered she'd left them with Redmond.

"Were you going to let me in or just stand there laughing all night?" she demanded crossly.

"I'd have let you in eventually. Maybe. If you asked nicely."

"Great, so now I need to ask nicely before I'm allowed into my own flat." Lisa's disgust showed in her voice and she didn't bother to fight it. "Remind me why I need a man in my life!"

"To rescue you from evil taxi drivers?" Redmond suggested.

Lisa wasn't sure it was in good taste to bring up the subject, but she had to admit Redmond was right. She'd have been pretty stuck without him there. She wasn't going to let him off that easily, though. As they made their way up the stairs, she threw a comment over her shoulder: "So I need a good man in my life to save me from all the bad men in my life? I think I'll just do without men in my life altogether."

"But just think what you'd be missing! Someone to dance with, fight with, make up with…"

Redmond trailed off as she walked into the flat, and the way he trained his eyes, hawk-like, on her face should have given her a clue to expect something out of the ordinary.

The table was laid out for dinner with the nearest to a matching set of crockery she possessed, and the crystal water jug she'd been given as a housewarming present and never used. In the centre of the table was the gigantic bouquet of red roses, now augmented with clouds of white gypsophila.

"Wow!"

"If you'd care to take a seat," Redmond invited, eyes sparkling, "dinner will be served shortly."

"What the…?" Lisa knew she wasn't at her most articulate, but she was too stunned to phrase the question more carefully.

Redmond laughed. "Sit down," he repeated, pulling out a chair for her. "I'll be back in a second."

He disappeared kitchen-wards and returned with two plates on which rolls of smoked salmon nestled in lettuce leaves, each topped with a neat wedge of lemon.

"That looks beautiful. You should have been a chef."

"Didn't you know? I almost was. I used to help out in the kitchen at Luca's sometimes in between shows, and he offered me a full-time job there when I finished college. If I hadn't got the offer from America, I'd probably have done it, but America paid so much better there was no contest."

Lisa raised her eyebrows. It had been hard to imagine Redmond as a waiter, but she wasn't sure if the idea of him slogging away in a hot industrial kitchen was more or less conceivable. One odd consequence of the revelation was that she felt embarrassed about her feeble efforts in the kitchen when Redmond came for dinner. She said as much.

"Why didn't you say?" she continued.

"I don't like mentioning it to people for exactly that reason," he explained. "It makes people get all self-conscious and apologetic about eating the way they would normally. And I don't want to eat restaurant food all the time—it's nice to get real meals sometimes, the sort of thing other people eat. Don't worry—I have my beans-on-toast evenings, too!"

If Lisa had thought for a moment that he was just being nice she'd have been furious at being patronised, but his heartfelt protestation had the ring of truth about it. Redmond knew what he liked, and wasn't afraid to say so. If he said he wanted soggy packet tortellini because that was what other people ate, then that was what he wanted.

"Anyway," he went on, "if I'd told you, you'd have expected something like this, and I wanted it to be a surprise."

"Mmm. I don't normally like surprises, but you can surprise me more often if they're all going to be like this." Lisa licked the lemon juice off her fingers. "No wonder you weren't worried about what was in the house to eat. But when on earth did you find time to do all this and find me a dress? Didn't you have work to do on that choreography for the advert today?"

"Nothing that wouldn't keep until tomorrow," he said lazily, leaning languidly back as far as the upright chair would permit.

"So what do you have to do tomorrow?" Lisa knew very little about his work life. It was one of the things she had meant to remedy, but so far she'd not had much of a chance.

Redmond's face became guilty and Lisa looked at him suspiciously as he answered, "Just some paperwork and a couple of meetings."

"So what aren't you telling me?"

The sheepish expression intensified. "What makes you think I'm not telling you something?"

"Your expression, for starters. You're a lousy liar. There is something, isn't there? There must be. Apart from anything else, when I said there was, you didn't deny it. If I was wrong, you'd have taken great delight in telling me so. So I'm right. Yes?"

Redmond shrugged awkwardly. "I wasn't going to tell you until after dinner. Let's talk about it later, OK?"

That aggravated Lisa. Now her dinner was going to be spoilt with the anticipation of bad news.

"Oh, I get it," she accused, "this was just a buttering up dinner. Making up for whatever you're about to say. Cheers very much. And there was me thinking maybe you'd actually just wanted to be nice for once. Thanks a bunch."

"For once? Well, that's charming too! Anyway, no, it wasn't. I'd already bought the stuff for dinner before I got the call. And believe me, if you weren't at the top of my agenda I wouldn't be here doing this. I'd be happily tucked up in bed by now getting a good night's sleep before getting up early in the morning to drive to the airport. No, on second thoughts, I'd probably already be on a plane so that I could get back and sleep in my own bed for at least some of the night."

"Airport?" Lisa was struggling to keep up. "You're going to America?"

"'Fraid so."

Lisa was petrified he was taking off for good again, but her hammering heart and short breath prevented her getting out the question. She swallowed hard and asked instead, "What for?"

"As I said, some meetings and some paperwork that needs my signature."

"But what about the competition?" It was the nearest she dared get to asking whether they had a future.

"I'll be back in time for the next round if everything goes according to plan."

"And if it doesn't?"

"Well, with transatlantic flights, just about anything can happen, but it mostly doesn't. I've only been delayed a couple of times, and never for more than a few hours. Even if the flight's a bit late, I can drive straight from the airport to the studio. Might be an idea if you take my costume and stuff in with you, though—I don't fancy taking them all the way to America and back. Besides, I trust you more than I trust BA's baggage handlers."

"Thanks. I think."

Lisa found herself grinning, though whether at his small joke or at the realisation that he wasn't intending to return to the States for good just yet, she wasn't sure.

"So am I forgiven?"

Lisa studied his face. He looked genuinely contrite. On the other hand, it wasn't the best news ever, nor had she particularly enjoyed the way he'd presented it to her. It wouldn't hurt to let him stew a bit longer, she decided.

"That depends."

"On what?"

She thought about it.

"How about you make it up to me?" she suggested.

"How would I do that?"

"Use your imagination!" Then, because that might have been a dangerous invitation, she clarified, "Dinner would be a good start. The salmon was fantastic, but I'm still hungry."

"Good," Redmond said, levering himself out of his chair with a look of relief which Lisa guessed related to the fact that she hadn't made more of a scene about him disappearing off to America.

While he was out of the room, Lisa wondered what had possessed her. She should be making a scene. After all, Redmond had stepped in at only a fortnight's notice to partner her for the show, and now he wasn't even going to be here for a crucial week of the series. Could they hope to get anywhere on the small amount of practice they had behind them?

Then she found herself grinning. She'd thought earlier that the competition wasn't the real point, and now she was paying for it. The universe must have decided to take her at her word.

Redmond came back in with two plates on one arm and a bottle in the other hand.

She wanted to ask what was on the plates, but somehow or other the maternal, fussy part of her mind got the upper hand.

"Tell me you're not drinking when you're going to be driving to the airport in... not very long." She'd meant to count the hours but realised she'd never found out the time of his flight.

"Seven hours," he supplied helpfully. "Don't worry—it's just sparkling grape juice. I want you sober tonight so I know it's not the cocktails talking."

"Why, do cocktails make a habit of starting conversations with you?" Lisa asked cheekily. Her heart was singing at the implications of his comment. It wasn't the kind of thing you'd say unless you had something more than just absent-minded chitchat planned. Maybe they'd get the chance to make up for last night—though not for long! Honestly, of all the times to come up with an urgent business trip! Couldn't it have waited?

Lisa bit her tongue. She didn't want to spoil their evening together with recriminations. He wouldn't be going if it weren't necessary... would he? Lisa had to admit she didn't know too much about how he thought. Every time she decided she had him sussed, he came out with something to surprise her. Like the mad flight of fancy he was now engaged in, chatting away to an imaginary Blue Lagoon. It was hilarious, yet somehow maddening. In seven hours he was going to disappear back off to the other side of the world, and here he was joking about drinks. She didn't want to waste a moment... but was it a waste to have a pleasant, enjoyable, normal evening? Perhaps not. She joined in his laughter as the imaginary conversation tailed off into unfocused hilarity.

"Sorry," Redmond said, and for a moment she thought he'd sensed her disapproval, but no, he was just apologising for keeping her chatting while their dinner got cold. She took the hint and tucked in. It was some kind of faintly spiced stew, reminiscent of what she'd enjoyed at Marrakech, and it was tasty enough to thoroughly distract her from both his silliness and the thought of his departure.

It was surprisingly filling and she ended up pushing her plate away still laden.

"You can't be full," Redmond protested. "What about dessert?"

"Maybe I could find room for a bite or two... in a minute..." Despite her sweet tooth, Lisa wasn't in any hurry for dessert. More food was the last thing she wanted right now. Instead they sat at the table drinking grape juice and chatting about irrelevant things: old school friends, fellow dancers, the weather in America, and the way American TV seemed to be taking over the British viewing schedules.

Finally Lisa found her mouth watering again at the thought of dessert.

Redmond grinned.

"I'll have to watch out, won't I? If I start encouraging you, you won't fit into any of your dresses when I come back. Mind you, that could have its advantages." He grinned, running his hand across her bare back as he passed her chair on his way to the kitchen.

Lisa stuck her tongue out at his departing back.

For a while, when they were just sitting at the table chatting, it had felt like old times, and she'd almost wondered if things were better that way. Their friendship was so easy and comfortable, she was afraid of how things would change as they got more involved. But Redmond's hands on her skin felt right too, at once exciting and gently reassuring. Surely anything that made her feel that way couldn't be a bad thing.

Redmond came back with a tray containing a complicated contraption that looked like a miniature camping stove, two forks, and a plate of marshmallows and chopped fruit. Lisa puzzled over the contraption for a few moments, then identified it tentatively as a fondue pan.

"Ever had a chocolate fondue?" Redmond asked, confirming her surmise.

"No." Lisa's puzzlement must have showed, because Redmond immediately demonstrated how to keep the little burner at the right temperature so that the chocolate remained soft, and then dipped a pineapple piece for her to try.

"Mmmm," Lisa closed her eyes and rolled the sweet, chocolatey fruit around in her mouth.

"Nice?"

"Do you need to ask?"

"Good. I'm glad you like it. By the way, you have chocolate round your mouth."

Lisa ran her tongue around her lips.

"Gone?"

"Not quite. Here." He put his hand on her shoulder to steady her—or himself, she wasn't sure—and leaned towards her, kissing and licking away the chocolate from the corner of her mouth.

When he finally released her, Lisa had to take a deep breath. "This has to be the best dessert anyone's ever made me." She smiled.

"Try a marshmallow," Redmond said, deflecting her praise almost as if it embarrassed him, though he wasn't usually shy about such things.

She speared a marshmallow and coated it thoroughly, but instead of taking it herself, she held it to his lips.

"Your turn," she insisted, and he leaned forward and took the sticky sweet in his mouth.

Then Lisa tried one, and was fascinated by the contrast between the fluffy centre and thick, smooth coating. Considering she had been full five minutes earlier, she seemed to have very little trouble fitting in the sweet fruit, but eventually she decided she'd had enough.

"One more," Redmond insisted, waving a chocolate-coated strawberry in her direction.

"No more," Lisa demurred, pressing her lips tightly together as he thrust the sweet towards them. She could feel the warm sauce smearing around her mouth, but was determined not to give in.

"Go on."

"No!" Foolishly, she opened her mouth to spit the word, and Redmond took advantage of the opportunity to press the fork between her lips. "Mmmmf," she found herself protesting, biting down sharply. Half the strawberry was in her mouth by this time, flooding her taste buds with sweetness. The other half disintegrated and dropped into her lap.

Redmond quickly removed the fallen fruit, but the chocolate had already made its mark on the light fabric.

"Oh no," Lisa wailed. "I should have known better than to eat dinner in a dress like this!"

"Don't worry," Redmond said, "if you soak it in cold water straight away the stain will probably come out. Besides, it's a dancing dress. Who's going to look that closely?"

"I'll know."

"Well, let's get it in some water. Have you got an old washing up bowl or something?"

Redmond put out the fondue burner and bustled her into the kitchen, where he filled the bowl with cold water and set it on the worktop.

She noticed in passing how tidy the place was compared to the previous occasion when she'd cooked—but then, she supposed, he'd had most of the afternoon to get it sorted out, whereas she'd only had half an hour.

Redmond swept her hair to one side and untied the halter neck of her dress. Lisa felt awkward. It wasn't the kind of dress you wore much underneath, and when Redmond slipped it over her head, she was left standing in just flimsy lace briefs and high heels. Redmond didn't make it any easier by keeping his eyes fixed on her as he plunged the dress into the cold water and swished it around.

Lisa tried not to squirm under his gaze. She was a dancer, for goodness sake! She wasn't supposed to be self-conscious about her body. Although she suspected that her discomfort was less to do with being looked at, than with the unaccustomed reaction it was eliciting. Her nipples were tightening, and in the heat of the kitchen she could hardly blame that on the temperature. It was entirely a response to Redmond, and to the way he looked at her, with a sensuous smile creeping across his face.

For a long moment they both just stood there, unmoving, and then, very slowly, he reached out and traced the curve of her breast. His finger, still damp from rinsing the dress, left a chilly trail behind it, so that his touch lingered even when his hand moved on. The water traced a cool path towards her nipple until she could no longer resist pressing harder against his hand and turning her face towards him to invite a kiss.

Redmond pressed his lips to hers, beginning a trail of kisses across her face, neck, and breasts until his tongue could take over where his fingers left off. Then his hands were free to roam all over her, stroking her back and pressing her still more closely against his body. Finally he settled with one hand in the small of her back, while he slid the fingers of his other hand inside her skimpy briefs, where they played gently and teasingly until she moaned with pleasure.

Lisa's hands were resting on the edge of the work surface, anchoring her as she stretched towards Redmond, pressing her mouth against his and playing her tongue over his lips and teeth, as his fingers played against her. Finally Redmond took a step away. Lisa looked up at him with a small whimper of disappointment, but before she could say anything he hooked his fingers through the elastic at her waist and slid her underwear gently to the floor.

"Now I feel silly wearing shoes," she remarked shakily, but Redmond made no move to remove them.

"But they make you the perfect height for this," Redmond explained, standing up and pressing the full length of his body against her, his lips seeking hers again. He was right. Their bodies matched perfectly; his hips locked against hers and the hardness of his erection pressed into her through the rough fabric of his trousers. His hands ran up and down her back, teasing her spine with little, fluttery strokes, then digging deeper into the muscles to release tensions she hadn't known were there.

Lisa had been leaning on both hands, but now she transferred her weight just to one, so that the other could reciprocate, tugging Redmond's shirt out of his trousers and playing across his back. Then Redmond pulled back again, so that her hands slid around his body to caress his waist and chest, while he kissed her neck and slid his hand back between her legs. This time, with nothing in the way, he was able to give her even more pleasure than before, and as she unbuttoned his shirt she looked down and saw his fingers sliding easily into her.

His touch was firmer now, and she found her body moving in response, so that she had to brace herself harder against the work surface with one hand, while the other tightened on his shoulder, guiding his head downwards until his lips reached her breast again.

"Ah," she gave a gasp of mixed pleasure and pain as his mouth tightened on her breast and his fingers thrust into her. Without meaning to, she found she'd echoed her words of the previous night: "I want you." This time there was no shyness attached, and she kept her eyes fixed on his face, seeing how he turned his face up towards her, his lips parted with an answering desire as he slowly withdrew his fingers, stood up, and lifted her effortlessly. She linked her arms around his neck, enjoying the feel of his bare chest against her skin where his shirt had caught open.

He negotiated the kitchen table carefully and took her out to the living room, where his eyes lit on the sofa. He set her along its length and then knelt at the end and unfastened her sandals. For some reason this amused Lisa.

"Oh, I am allowed to take them off, then," she said. "I was beginning to think you had some kind of shoe fetish."

"Well, now you mention it," Redmond teased, but he chucked the sandals to one side and concentrated instead on kissing the hollow by her ankle bone. She was astonished how good it felt and how sensitive the skin was there. However, Redmond soon moved on, kissing up her calves and the insides of her thighs, and licking gently at the hollows of her hips. Again she found herself arching her back in pleasure and running her fingers through his hair and across his shoulders. She kept catching on his collar, however, and she soon pushed him upright and tugged off his shirt.

"Don't feel you have to stop there." He smiled, so she ran her hand shyly downwards and unfastened his trousers. He helped her out by pulling off his socks and stepping out of his trousers, but waited for her to take the final step and help him out of his shorts. Now that she could see his whole body, she marveled still more at his hard leanness. He perched on the edge of the sofa, running his hands over her body and letting her hands play all over him.

Redmond cleared his throat awkwardly. Lisa raised her eyebrows. That wasn't like him at all.

"Sorry to be boringly practical," he said, sounding embarrassed, "but I have to ask. Are you on the pill or anything?"

Lisa shook her head. She'd never needed to worry about pills, because Brandon the control freak hadn't trusted her with their protection – that probably should have told her something about their 'relationship'. Since then, she hadn't even thought about having condoms in the house. Lisa presumed Redmond would have thought further ahead than her. It seemed, from his rummaging in a trouser pocket and digging into his wallet, that she was right.

He sat with his back to her as he slipped on the condom. She ran her hands hungrily over his back and tried not to think too hard about the fact that finally all her wildest dreams were coming true, or the equally strange fact that in just hours he would once again be disappearing from her life.

Then Redmond kissed her once, deeply, and lowered himself gently between her legs, and there was no chance to think about anything at all.

Redmond was, as she'd come to expect, a gentle, considerate lover, and their lovemaking was everything she'd hoped—but hardly dared to expect—that it would be.

Afterwards, Lisa curled up sleepily, her head in his lap, until Redmond asked curiously, "Aren't you cold?"

"No." Lisa smiled up at him, a wide, satisfied smile. "I'm still pretty warm. How about you?"

"I'm cooling off a bit," he admitted.

"Warmer in bed," she said drowsily, so Redmond picked her up again and deposited her amongst the covers before sliding in beside her and giving her a gentle kiss on the forehead.

Lisa barely noticed him setting the alarm. She woke up just enough to smile at the thought that it was supposed to be men who turned over afterwards and fell asleep, but before she could get around to explaining the joke to Redmond, drowsiness had overtaken her again.

Chapter 11

When Lisa woke, the window was just beginning to lighten with the dawn, and Redmond was once again sleeping peacefully beside her. She didn't seem to want to sleep anymore. Instead, her mind replayed the evening over and over again, reveling in the strange new sensation of Redmond here beside her. He seemed to fit as nobody else ever had, perhaps because she'd always been somehow comparing everyone else with the dream she'd had of a future with Redmond, before he'd disappeared. Nobody else had ever lived up to it. Perhaps he wouldn't either, but at least she'd know. And if this ended, perhaps she'd find herself finally free of him. She didn't relish the thought.

Was there something wrong with her, to be thinking like this after the passion they'd shared the night before? She cast her mind back. Doubts like this certainly hadn't been in her mind then.

As she remembered Redmond moving inside her, she found her body responding again, and Redmond, as if aware of this, turned over in his sleep and pressed closer to her. Lisa tentatively laid a hand on his hip, and he arched against it. She snuggled closer to him again and settled back on the pillow to await sleep, but instead she found herself lying awake, noticing the warm weight of Redmond's arm draped over her. She opened her eyes to find him leaning over her watchfully, and when he saw her awake he reached down and kissed her.

"Shouldn't you be asleep?" she asked.

"Shouldn't you?"

"I don't need to be up so early."

"I can sleep on the plane."

Lisa shrugged. She wasn't going to argue when she could be enjoying his closeness.

All in all, it was a perfect night, only spoiled when the alarm eventually shrilled, startling Lisa so that, to Redmond's amusement, she jumped dramatically.

"Do you really have to go?" Lisa asked pitifully, in a reversal of the previous day's parting scene.

"Afraid so. I'll make sure I'm back in plenty of time for filming, though."

"How much time?" Lisa didn't trust plane schedules. She'd once been held up for twenty-four hours just getting back from Ireland.

"Plenty," Redmond said firmly. "The flight gets in at lunchtime, and I'll go straight to the studio. I'll be there hours early. Probably before you."

"As long as your flight's on time."

"If it isn't, there's another one two hours later. They're like buses, these planes."

Strangely, the thought didn't inspire Lisa with confidence, but she knew when to call it quits. Redmond was downplaying the risk, and she just had to hope he was right. Panicking wouldn't change anything, anyway.

"Shall I come with you to the airport?" she suggested instead.

"No point. I need to pop back to the flat first to pick up my bags and the car, and it'll hardly take me any time to drive down."

"Do you want anything before you go? Breakfast? Tea?"

"I'll get something at the airport."

"Sure there's nothing I can do?"

"Give me a kiss?"

So she did. A long, slow, langurous, teasing kiss that made her wish doubly that he wasn't leaving.

Walking to work, Lisa was lifted by the memory of that kiss. Despite the autumn chill, she floated happily down the street to the bus stop. The sun, low in the sky, illuminated her breath in front of her face, and made the frosty pavement sparkle like glittery stage makeup. It was as if the world was putting on its party clothes ready for Christmas. Even the discarded cuddly dog sitting on a neighbour's wall looked cheeky and alert rather than bedraggled. And the final touch was the display of bright tropical flowers blooming on one of the flats' balconies, which puzzled Lisa until she realised that the flamboyant orange and blue blossoms were plastic.

Everybody just seemed to have decided to have fun that day, and although Lisa was sad to lose Redmond for days, so early in their real relationship, a small practical part of her mind had already observed that five days without extra dancing meant five days in which to catch up at work and get herself out of trouble.

If only it had worked like that.

In Redmond's absence, he suddenly became ten times more absorbing than when he was actually there. He texted occasionally, but the messages were sweet without giving anything away, and when she plucked up the courage to risk transatlantic mobile charges and call him, his mobile was switched off. In the absence of a phone call, she found herself reading the texts over and over again, looking for hidden meanings, although it was tough to derive much from, "Keep smiling! Looking forward to dancing – and other things – at the weekend. X, Red."

At her desk, she'd sit twiddling her pen and thinking about his kisses. In meetings, a word or phrase would trigger the memory of one of his jokes, and then she'd find the corners of her mouth twitching at inappropriate moments. Just to make matters worse, "Ghastly Gary"—as the girls in the office had taken to calling him behind Alan's back—didn't like any of the three designs because they failed to reflect an aspect of the original brief that Lisa couldn't remember ever being discussed. She was pretty sure he'd made it up after the event, but without proof, she didn't dare imply that he was lying or mistaken. So it was back to the drawing board.

The next set of designs took most of the week, and it was late on Friday when Lisa fired off the final pictures to Gary. She followed them up with a disgusted email to Marian commenting on how long the designs had taken and what the chances were of Ghastly Gary actually approving them this time, and then headed home to her empty flat.

After assembling an easy tea from the random leftovers in the fridge, Lisa found herself noticing the silence as she ate. She turned on the radio and discovered it was still tuned to Radio Two from when she'd last had workmen in. Being too lazy to retune it, she hummed along to some cheesy disco hit, and pondered why the silence had suddenly started disturbing her. Normally, with her hectic schedule of work, teaching, and practice, she was grateful for some quiet time, but now she didn't like being alone with her thoughts. She'd come to enjoy sharing easy banter with Red over dinner, but in his absence all the doubts came flooding back. Sure, his texts sounded cheery enough, and he still said he was looking forward to seeing her, but what if absence didn't make his heart grow fonder? Would he rediscover the joys of America now that he'd spent some time away, and regret having to come back to her?

She could do with someone to talk to, and although Red had warned her that he'd be in meetings most of the day, she was still frustrated to find his phone off again. After hanging up from the fourth attempt, she dumped the mobile back in her handbag and went for the landline instead, but when she thought about the other people she could call, she realised how badly she'd been ignoring all her friends since the show started. Well, she'd had some excuse, and they were too nice to start hating her for it, but now that she had a free evening, it was a good time to try catching up.

Her first thought was to call Terri, but she'd finally trained herself to recall that dinnertime in her world was bedtime in baby world, and she didn't want to risk disturbing the household routine, so she made a mental note to call in the morning instead.

In the meantime, she could try Jerry, though she didn't rate her chances of catching him at home. It was, after all, Friday night, and Friday night was party time.

As she'd expected the phone rang and rang, but if she waited the answerphone would kick in and she could at least leave a message to say she'd thought of him. But when a slight click eventually signaled the connection being made, she was greeted with a breathless "Hello."

"Oh, hi," she said, flustered by finding herself talking to the real thing instead of a recorded voice.

"Hi. You sound surprised. Who did you think you were ringing?"

"I thought you'd be out. Are you feeling OK?"

"Well, the crutches do cramp my style a bit down at the Cav. Though I have to admit, they're handy for defence if anyone seems to be thinking about indulging in a bit of gay-bashing."

Lisa laughed.

"I didn't expect to hear from you tonight, either," Jerry observed. "Where's lover boy?"

"America." Lisa couldn't help sounding doleful.

"And he didn't take you?" There was a pause as Jerry realised his mistake. "Well, no, I guess not. You wouldn't have wanted to go, though, would you?"

"No, but it's nice to be asked."

"He didn't ask you? The way you two look at each other, I thought you couldn't bear to be apart for more than a few seconds."

"It didn't occur to you that we might be faking for the cameras?"

"Give me some credit. I've been on the receiving end of your fake adoring looks. I'd recognise them a mile off. Whatever you and Red say, or think, you two are for real, so don't give me any of that rubbish."

"Yeah, OK, so it's not all fake, but... oh, I don't know... it's all so weird. I could so do without this show," Lisa said, although come to think of it the show was the whole reason they were together, so wishing it away did seem a bit hypocritical.

"Sounds like a two bottle evening," Jerry said, and Lisa smiled in spite of herself.

"I'll get a taxi and bring a bottle round, shall I?" For a moment, the thought of getting in a taxi terrified her, but she wasn't going to give in to an irrational fear. Still, she made sure to call the local firm she'd been using for five years, and ask for one of their familiar drivers.

After a few minutes' chat with the driver, she felt more relaxed. Maybe she wouldn't even need the second bottle of wine when she got to Jerry's. Though, come to think of it, that had never stopped them before.

She had to juggle her handbag and the cold wine bottle to open the front door, which Jerry buzzed for her. Normally he came down, but she could appreciate that with the crutches it was a little trickier than usual.

"So what's new with you?" she asked as she set out wine glasses and poured, letting Jerry remain with his foot up on the sofa. "How's, um, thingybob?" She'd given up trying to remember names, and it never seemed to offend Jerry. Not that much ever did.

"Fine, I think, but it's not going anywhere between us. That's fine with me, though. I've got other things to think about."

"Oh, are you in love again?" Lisa asked, trying not to sound cynical. Just because her own love life had always been a disaster, was no reason to expect Jerry's should be the same. One day he'd find some perfect guy and settle down to a lifetime of pipes and slippers, or whatever represented cosy domesticity for gay men. Maybe it was in the air at the moment, because Lisa's life was certainly looking rosier than it had for a long time.

"In love?" For once Jerry seemed to be thinking about the question instead of just launching into a paean of praise to his latest fancy. "I don't know. There's someone… he's pretty special… but it's complicated."

"Complicated?" This was a new departure for Jerry, whose relationships had typically been limited to simple unrequited, or occasionally requited, lusts.

"Yes. He's… well, he's not out."

"But he is interested?"

"I think so. I mean, it's obvious he's bent, if you know what to look for, but nobody else seems to know, and the papers would have a field day if they found out. He'd be in a shitload of trouble."

"The papers?" Lisa seemed to be losing her grip on the conversation and stupidly echoing everything Jerry said. But where on earth had he found someone the papers would have a field day with? She tried to imagine Jerry involved with a politician, a film star, a pop singer, someone the tabloids regularly dished the dirt on, but the image refused to gel. For all his flashy style and pretence at the wild life, Jerry was a gentle home lover, and it was impossible to imagine him the eye-candy partner of a media-hungry celebrity.

Lisa had never liked the media, and her involvement with *Couples* had only served to cement her distaste for their shallowness. And now Jerry was getting interested in somebody who the papers would hang out to dry if they got wind of the relationship. This wasn't good.

"Jerry, who is this guy?"

There was a long pause. Jerry looked down at the table, then over Lisa's left shoulder. He stirred his coffee, took a sip, and put the cup down again. Finally, when Lisa had begun to think he wasn't going to tell her, and to wonder whether maybe it would be easier if she never knew, he took a long slow breath and answered, "It's… Fritz."

The silence after he had spoken stretched even longer and more awkwardly than the one before. "He's…" Lisa began finally, and then paused as she wondered where to begin objecting. He's… what? Straight? Maybe not. Now that Lisa thought about it, he and Kathrin seemed to have a pleasantly comradely relationship not at all like Harry and Tiffany's cool, suppressed passion or the Braithwaites' blatant affection. There was something a little odd about it, and about Fritz's manner around the other guys on the show—he always seemed to be holding back a little. There was more emotion in his eyes than his words had ever seemed to express, but Lisa had always assumed that was because English was his second language.

He's… OK, gay made sense, but… wasn't he with Kathrin? Did she know? Was she colluding in the fantasy, or had he fooled her along with the TV crew and the papers?

No wonder Jerry said the media would have a field day.

"He's in the show. With Kathrin. Jerry, you can't ruin that for him." Whatever else, Fritz and Kathrin seemed like decent people. There was the small matter of lying about his sexuality, of course, but Lisa couldn't exactly take the moral high ground on that one.

"Of course not," Jerry said, outraged at the suggestion that he would take risks with Fritz's happiness. "But maybe after the show…"

Lisa almost wished she could fast forward for six weeks. She had the sense that a lot of things were going to be different after the show.

But then, after the show, she still hadn't lost the sense that Redmond might just disappear back into the Florida sunshine. When he was in her life and her bed, it felt real, but right now there was an ocean between them, and she found it hard to imagine a future after the end of the show. No matter how much sense it made, she couldn't wish that moment closer.

"Maybe…" Lisa agreed slowly. "But Fritz? How on earth did that happen?"

Jerry spread his hands out, a slow gesture indicating his

bewilderment. "I don't know. He's just… a really sweet guy, you know. Seeing him at the filming of the show, and you know they demo at the dances at the Carlton, where I take my sister sometimes?" Lisa had forgotten Jerry had been at the filming, and she hadn't known about where Fritz and Kathrin did demos, but she knew of the dances at the Carlton, so she nodded anyway to indicate her familiarity. She didn't want to break up Jerry's unusually serious confiding mood by asking more questions.

"Well, anyway, I don't know. I don't suppose anything will come of it. But I can still enjoy him from afar. There's no harm in that, is there?"

Lisa shook her head, but privately she wondered. She'd spent years loving Redmond from afar, and all it had done was spoiled her for anyone else. It certainly hadn't made things any easier once he'd come back on the scene.

"I don't suppose so," she agreed. Then something, possibly the wine, made her continue. "Sometimes I wish that was all I'd done."

"Really? I thought everything was all sweetness and light now. Or is that just another act for the cameras?"

"I don't know." Lisa couldn't believe she was opening herself up like this, but at least it was to someone she could trust. If she'd tried to bottle things up much longer, she wouldn't have been surprised if she ended up spilling her story to one of the camera crew, and then where would she be?

Somehow the process of hearing what she'd said, and reasoning with herself about how much more she could safely reveal, resulted in a long pause in the conversation. That was probably also down to the wine, she thought muzzily. "Sometimes it just seems so perfect. And sometimes it seems too perfect. You know, as if I must be dreaming. What the hell would 'Mr. Cosmopolitan travelled the world and danced with beautiful women from six continents' want with little me? And I just know I'm going to wake up like Cinderella after the ball, but nobody's going to come round with a glass slipper."

"Lisa, Lisa," Jerry said, shaking his head sorrowfully. "What are we going to do with you? You should know you could compete with anyone on any continent. As a dancer, and as a person. Why, sometimes you even make me wish I was straight."

"Thanks, I think." Lisa smiled, and held out her glass for a top-up. Thank goodness she could always rely on Jerry to make her feel better. Why on earth couldn't straight men be so uncomplicated?

"So tell me the important bit," Jerry continued, unperturbed by her reaction to his compliment. "What is it about Redmond? I mean, OK, I can see the appeal of the football player physique, but there's got to be more to it than that. Muscles alone don't melt the heart of a discerning lady like yourself."

Lisa laughed and shook her head, but she still gave the question the attention it deserved. Oddly, she'd never really thought about what made Redmond so special. She'd just taken it for granted that he was. Maybe it was just because he acted as if he thought he was special, but surely she couldn't be so easily swayed by a classic case of masculine arrogance?

After a moment, Lisa concluded, "Well, yes, it's his looks, but also who he is. He's good fun to be around. And caring."

"And I'm not?" Jerry asked, looking mock woebegone.

Lisa didn't deign to answer that. Instead, she added, deadpan, "And heterosexual." Then she added, surprising even herself, "Not to mention great in bed."

Jerry spluttered out a laugh. "Lisa! I'm shocked!"

Lisa looked at him all wide-eyed innocence. "What? We're all grown-ups. I didn't think you were so easily shocked."

Jerry smiled. "I was just surprised. You don't normally say things like that."

Lisa forbore from answering that she also didn't normally get to go to bed with guys quite as amazing as Redmond. That might have led to more detail than Jerry needed to know.

Instead, she let the conversation drift back to safer topics, and eventually the last of the wine had been consumed and she reluctantly made a move to call a taxi and head home.

*

Back in her empty flat, she couldn't believe how quickly she'd got used to having company around the place. After two nights of Redmond's presence, her bed felt cold and empty, and the living room was so silent she thought she could hear the echoes of her footsteps when she walked through it. As for the kitchen, she hardly dared go in there, because everything about it taunted her: memories of Redmond's caresses, the novelty of cooking real food, and even the taste of chocolate accentuated her loneliness. So now she knew what it would be like if Redmond went back to America to live, and she wasn't enjoying the thought.

Since the oversleeping disaster she'd been rigorous about setting her alarm, to the point that on Saturday it woke her at seven even though she didn't need to be up for hours.

She turned on the radio as soon as she got into the kitchen. The announcer was wittering about yesterday's TV, and Lisa half-listened as she boiled the kettle and poured herself a mug of tea. She understood logically about the dehydrating effect of alcohol, but it still struck her as bizarre that the more you drank, the more you needed to drink.

After a few mouthfuls of tea, she realised it was time for some breakfast, and dumped two slices of bread in the toaster. While sipping tea and waiting for the toast, she was surprised to hear her own name. She looked at the radio in surprise, as if to ask it what it meant by addressing her directly. The announcer was talking about the *Couples* show. Somehow, Lisa had managed to forget that the first episode had aired on Friday. Thinking back, she realised it had been on when she was catching the taxi over to

Jerry's. He must have just finished watching it when she arrived. Or perhaps he'd recorded it for later. She must text him and find out if it was still on his recorder. Given that his latest crush was in it, she'd happily bet that it was.

She was thinking this with only half her mind, though. The rest was set on trying to reconstruct from the last few words what the announcer was saying about the show. He seemed to be generally positive, and sympathetic to Lisa for the "accident," which he stopped just short of suggesting was deliberate sabotage. Still, the hint of an accusation was there, and Lisa was pleased that Tiffany's insults didn't seem to be taking hold. Surely nobody believed Lisa and Red would have been so clumsy as to dance into Tiffany and Harry's path.

Lisa belatedly realised that she hadn't checked for messages last night when she got in. She took her tea into the lounge and pressed play, then took the phone with her to the kitchen when she realised there were half a dozen messages to listen to.

The first was Terri, congratulating her on Redmond and the show and suggesting she ring around lunchtime one day for a proper chat.

The second was Red himself, saying hi from America and confirming that he was still due back on Saturday and should see her at the studio. She wished he'd rung before she went out. Hearing his voice made her realise how sad it was not to be sharing the first week of the show with him.

The third message was a man's voice, but he didn't identify himself immediately.

"Lisa?" The speaking voice sounded: cold and formal yet familiar. It took Lisa a second to place it, and then her heart sank. Alan. A call from your boss after you'd left work on a Friday night was never a good thing. At best it meant extra work. At worst, disaster.

"Lisa, I tried your mobile but you weren't picking up. Please call me as soon as you get this message." He left his mobile number, presumably not realising it was ingrained in Lisa's mind anyway.

The fourth message was Marian, ringing to say she'd seen the show and Lisa and Red looked fantastic. She could quite see what Lisa saw in Redmond. Lucky lady!

Lisa didn't feel lucky at the moment. She felt tired and headachy and full of foreboding, especially when the fifth message proved to be Alan again, hoping he hadn't misdialed the first time and leaving his number again.

What did Gary want now? She was sure it had to be something to do with Gary. He was nothing but trouble.

Lisa took the toast out of the toaster, but decided she needed to get the call over with sooner rather than later. She dialed Alan's mobile and he answered immediately.

"Do you have any idea what you've done?"

This was disaster, then. She racked her brains. She'd managed to get away with the lateness earlier in the week, and since then she thought she'd been on her best behaviour. Well, apart from grumbling a bit about Gary, but that was only to be expected. He was the world's worst client. But she'd only done it aloud when Alan was well and truly out of earshot. Well, and that one email...

And then, a split second before the words came out of Alan's mouth, she realised. One email complaining to Marian about Gary, typed in a hurry at the end of a long and depressing day. One email which she only now recalled seeing disappear into the ether with Gary's too-familiar email address at the top. Surely she hadn't typed his address out of sheer force of habit?

"Only bloody sent an email to the client slagging him off and using an insulting nickname," Alan ranted. So that answered her question. She had sent it to Gary, not Marian. "Honestly, Lisa, I've never heard of anything so unprofessional. I've thought you've been a bit off form lately, but this is something else entirely. I'm sorry, but I can't have staff jeopardising our reputation in this way. Gary's out for blood so unless you've got a very good explanation, don't bother coming in on Monday. Marian will be handling the account from now on. I'll be kind and call it redundancy, so you'll get pay in lieu of notice and as nice a reference as I dare under the circumstances. As I say, I'm sorry it's turned out like this, but I can't risk Gary turning up and finding you still in the office."

Lisa wanted to cry, scream, and demand he hear her side of the story, but the truth was that there was no other side, and they both knew it.

"Sorry, Alan," she said heavily. "I know it was stupid. I wasn't thinking."

"You can say that again," he said, sounding no happier at the situation than she was. "I'll clear your desk for you on Monday. Is there anything you need?"

She thought about it, and concluded that she could well live without the cough sweets, old makeup, and tissues that had been the only things in her desk she actually owned. The address book and diary belonged to the company anyway, as did the stack of *Marketing Week* magazines, although she could have done with those for job hunting. The thought threatened to set tears off, so she hastily turned down the offer and rang off.

Alan assured her that HR would be in touch. She wasn't looking forward to it.

She curled up in the corner of the sofa and stared at the floor. How could she have been so stupid? She knew exactly what she'd done; had realised it even before Alan told her. But why? Her mind had just been somewhere else all week.

And now, as if the competition, saving the studio, and starting a long-distance relationship were not enough to worry about, she had to find another job. Oh God, where to start?

Chapter 12

Stunned by her news, Lisa didn't know quite what to do for the next three hours. She'd thought of logging into her work emails and clearing a few overdue tasks, but there didn't seem much point now, so she settled for cleaning the kitchen. Sometimes when the world was in chaos, it was a comfort to restore order in a small way.

She emptied the accumulated rubbish of the last two weeks into a bin bag and lugged it out to the bin shed at the back of the car park. The air was thick with fog, and she wondered what it would be like for Redmond coming back to this. From Florida sunshine, he'd be stepping off the plane to air so moist you could almost feel the liquid on your tongue. In the car headlights on the road outside, she could see the drops swirling like angel dust. It was the kind of morning that meant if you were in the right mood you could believe in magic—ghosts coming through the mist, figures seen out of the corner of your eye that dissolved as soon as you looked at them. But the magic wasn't always benign. The red taillights of passing traffic had a devilish feel. Or maybe that was just Lisa's mood.

On the plus side, if she didn't have to go to the office all week, she might just have time to fit in some daytime dancing practice and visit her neglected juniors in the evenings. On the down side, she'd have to start worrying about how to pay the bills. She wasn't sure whether her newfound celebrity status was going to help or hinder her job search. It certainly didn't make her look like the most serious professional in the office. She hadn't thought through the implications of the show on her career, and she wondered whether she'd have made a different decision if she had. Now, though, it was almost impossible to imagine going back to life as it had been. The only way was forward, and for some reason that started with wiping down the surfaces in the kitchen and then, while she was on a roll, dusting the tops of the cupboards.

The phone rang while she was teetering on a chair with a rag in her hand. She considered not coming down to answer it, on the grounds that if there was any more bad news she didn't want to hear it, but then the feeling of suspense and dread about the possible bad news was worse than anything she was likely to hear. She scrambled down and picked up the phone just as the answer machine kicked in.

"Are we still OK to pick you up after lunch?" Elaine asked.

Elaine and Mark were determined to come to every filming session and watch their star students. Lisa wasn't entirely happy about that—she'd be less worried about messing up with an audience of strangers than with her beloved teachers in the front row—but she'd decided there was little she could do about it. It was, after all, a public event. Anyone could attend who wanted to, so there was no point in quarrelling. She might as well accept the lift.

"Sure," she agreed, and when she'd established that was all Elaine wanted, she rang off quickly, not wanting to get into too much conversation in case she let herself go and start talking about work and her worries. She'd do her best to keep it out of her mind until after the show. And cleaning was a great distraction. Terri would just have to wait until tomorrow for a phone call, too. She'd understand.

Having finished with the surfaces, Lisa hauled the hoover out from the cupboard and began on the floors. So she didn't hear the door buzzer until a long tone intruded on the vacuum's steady hum. Someone had evidently been buzzing for a while, and had finally started leaning on the entry phone in desperation.

Lisa looked at the clock on the video. Elaine was early.

She wiped a sleeve across her eyes, scooped up her shoe bag and costume carriers, and trotted downstairs.

Outside the door, Elaine's burgundy people-carrier was nowhere to be seen. Instead, Redmond was leaning on the lowered window of the now-familiar sports car. She ran to him, then realised that greeting him through a car window with an armful of bags was well nigh impossible. He popped the catch on the boot, got out to help her pile in the dresses, and then folded her into an embrace she thought would never end.

Finally he held her back at arm's length and inspected her tear-stained face. She wished she'd known he was coming so she could have tidied herself up more, then chided herself for the thought. She should look after herself, whether or not she expected Redmond to see her.

"What's up?" he asked.

She shook her head. "You don't want to know," she choked out. "What are you doing here anyway? Elaine was meant to be coming for me. Does she know?"

"Yes to the last question. I got bumped from my flight but I managed to get moved to an earlier one, so I called her from the airport to say I'd pick you up on my way by. They'll see us up there."

"Thanks," she said weakly, letting him open the door for her and help her into the low seat.

"You're welcome."

He walked round to the driver's side, settled in, and started the engine before raising the subject again.

"So come on, tell Uncle Redmond what's the matter."

She grimaced. He sounded so ridiculously cheesy, though he'd probably done it on purpose to try and make her smile.

"I don't want to talk about it. Not till after the show, at least."

"If you don't, I'll be forced to regale you with the excitement of my flight details instead," he threatened.

"Go ahead."

"Oh dear, it must be bad!"

"It is." Tears prickled at her eyes again and she blinked them away, hoping Redmond wouldn't see. If he did notice, he said nothing, just waited.

Eventually the silence became too painful, and Lisa found herself blurting out, "I lost my job."

Saying the words somehow made them even more real and terrifying. It was the kind of thing that should happen to other people. Not to smart, star performers, which until a few weeks ago, Lisa had considered herself—and, she thought, had been considered by others.

"Why? How?"

Lisa thought for a moment how to explain the situation, then gave him a brief summary, not trying to shift the blame because she was well aware the fault was her own.

To her surprise, Redmond laughed out loud.

"It's not funny! It's a disaster!"

Her protest became a wail and then she was crying again. It was getting to be a habit. This time Redmond couldn't do much because he was driving, but when they paused at the lights he handed her a tissue and gave her hair a brief stroke.

"It's a problem," Redmond conceded quietly. "But you have to admit it is quite funny. The guy sounds like he deserved it."

"That's just it," Lisa sniffed. "He deserved trouble but I got it. He's the client so he's right even when he's being obnoxious, and if I dare to say he's being obnoxious, then I get fired."

"Which isn't technically legal. You haven't been warned first or anything."

"They'll wriggle out of it somehow. They're calling it redundancy."

"Which means you get paid?"

"Not much, though."

"Better than nothing."

"True."

"Hey, don't worry. It'll get sorted. You'll see."

"Sorted how? I can't imagine Alan ringing next week to offer me my job back."

"I can't imagine you'd take it if he did. Next week you'll be trying to decide which top studio to take a teaching job with."

"If we don't get kicked out."

"What's happened to that confidence you used to have? Of course we can win. Tell me honestly, who's better than us? Nobody!"

"Not normally, but I'm not normal at the moment. Normally nobody's better than me at work either, and look at me now!"

"That's different," Redmond said, calmly and rationally. "You've been concentrating on your dancing, so you took your eye off the ball a bit in the office. That's understandable. But your work's only suffered because your dancing's improved. So if you were good before, you should be unbeatable now."

"After we've had almost a week without practicing together?"

Redmond nodded. "That's why I kept throwing in new things when we started dancing together again. I needed to be sure you could pick things up quickly and run with them, because I knew we wouldn't have much time to prepare for this week."

Lisa's mind wasn't working quickly, but it got there in the end.

"Hang on," she objected, "you said you only got the call that day. So how come you knew to test me before that?"

"I only got the call that day, but I had an idea this might come up. I'd been working on a deal and I shouldn't have left it when I did to come over here, but, as I said, the competition seemed like an unmissable opportunity."

"Some time," Lisa said, attempting to sound light, "you'll have to tell me about all these deals of yours." The "international man of mystery" act was beginning to wear a bit thin, and she wanted to know more about Redmond's life. She'd have asked him outright, but she was afraid he'd refuse to tell her, and she didn't want to row with him about it when so much depended on their getting on well. It was yet another conversation to add to the list of things they'd have to face up to after the show.

As Lisa had expected, Redmond grinned mysteriously. "All in good time, my dear," he said.

"Did you know you can be infuriatingly patronising at times?"

"I do now."

"Good."

"Although that may not be the best thing to say to someone who's giving you a lift across London out of the kindness of his heart. Keep it up and you might find yourself walking."

"Keep up the patronising tone and I might be glad to!"

"All right, I'm sorry. It was mean of me, I know, but I'd rather not talk about it until things are a bit more definite. Is that OK? I just worry about jinxing things, and it's all looking a bit shaky as it is."

"I won't ask anymore, then, but do tell me when you can, won't you?"

"Of course."

There was a pause as they both cast about for a safe topic of conversation, and then Redmond threw caution to the winds.

"So are you going to be OK? You sound pretty upset about this job thing."

That's putting it mildly, Lisa thought, but the truth was, given a bit of time, she could see that what he'd said was true. Her focus lately had been elsewhere, and a year ago that wouldn't have happened. So maybe the whole situation was telling her it was time for a change.

"I think so," she said instead, settling for a note of cautious optimism. "I don't quite know what I'm going to do, but I guess I'll figure something out."

"Good for you," Redmond encouraged.

"You don't sound too worried about it all."

"Of course not. I know it's been a big shock for you, but you're tough and smart. To be honest, I don't think you'd do something like that entirely by accident. I reckon maybe your subconscious had decided you were in a bit of a rut and decided to do something to shake you loose."

"Thanks, Dr. Freud," Lisa said sharply. "Remind me when you got your psychology degree?"

Underneath, though, she couldn't help wondering if he might have a point. Even before Redmond's arrival and the debacle at work, she remembered feeling a little restless and unsettled. Once or twice at work she'd created a really great layout and then found herself looking at it with irritation instead of satisfaction, thinking that there should be something more to life. New directions, new possibilities. And now she had them in spades: Redmond, dancing, and the search for a new job to look forward to.

"Sorry," Redmond said, sounding for once in his life almost genuinely contrite. "That was probably out of line. I tend to say what I think."

"No, really?" Lisa had forgotten how much she missed having someone forthright around, and being able to trust that she'd get an honest opinion.

"Do you mind?"

"Not if you don't mind me doing the same," Lisa said, though in truth she'd never be quite as forthright as Redmond. Still, it was nice not to have to watch her tongue too much. Though, as she'd already learned, honesty could be a dangerous habit to settle into.

"I don't know," Redmond said, though his grin suggested that any objections would only be in jest. "It depends what you're going to say. Try me."

Lisa thought for a moment. "Did you miss me?"

"Didn't have much time to," Redmond admitted. "I had to pack a lot in to get back here in time. But it was strange not to have someone to talk to about the day, and my bed felt pretty empty at night… for about three seconds before I crashed out. You have no idea how exhausting back to back meetings and flights can be."

"And you flew in this morning, and now you're driving. Is this a good idea?"

"I'm fine. If I get tired, we'll stop. But it's easy enough driving in London. Nothing goes at more than ten miles an hour, so even my slow reactions can handle it. So I'm fine for now, and I'll get over my jet lag during the week."

"You make it sound so easy."

"Isn't it?"

"Nothing's ever that easy." Lisa sighed, thinking of how complicated her life seemed to have become.

"You're too young to be such a cynic," Redmond said. He grinned as if he was joking but Lisa had the impression he meant it more seriously than he'd like to admit.

She thought about it.

"It's not easy, though, is it? Wanting things doesn't mean you get them. If it was that easy we could wave a magic wand and sort things out for Mark and Elaine, and I wouldn't be stuck here and you in America, and I wouldn't be out of a job for making the mistake of being honest for once."

Redmond looked as if he was about to say something, but when he opened his mouth it was only to remark that they were passing a very nice little café, and ask if she'd like to stop?

Much as she wanted to continue the conversation, she decided it would be better to make use of the ladies' toilets in the café to clean her face so that she didn't arrive scruffy and smeared with tears. By the time she got back to the car, Redmond seemed to have decided that the moment for serious conversation had passed. They spent the rest of the journey listening to the radio, although Redmond looked deep in concentration, either on the road or on his thoughts, so Lisa wasn't sure how much he heard.

"Are you sure you're OK?" Lisa asked as they made their way through to the studio. "You must be exhausted."

"Well, I have to admit those big sofas look quite appealing. But I'll be fine when we're dancing. The music always gives me a lift."

She knew what he meant. She felt the same. Once the beat got into your body, you came alive.

"Good."

They reached the dressing rooms, and Lisa reached up to give Redmond a quick kiss before going to get ready. She was already settling into the routine of getting into her makeup and whatever dress had been left for her. Today's was a skimpy silver Latin dress not totally unlike the one Redmond had brought for her to practice in on Wednesday. She flushed as she remembered where that had led, and forced herself to return her attention to the dress and the dance. The dress was short, but fringed with tassels which added a little to the length, and slightly reminiscent of a 1920s cocktail dress. It would be perfect for their cheeky, Charleston-ish steps, and she silently blessed the costume department.

Caroline, spectacular in a short red dress with a jeweled belt, gave Lisa's hand a squeeze as she passed. Lisa smiled up at her. Thank heavens for one friendly face. Tiffany had been lurking nearby since they came in, and it was surely only a matter of time before she opened her mouth and said something that set Lisa fuming.

As if on cue, Tiffany looked over at the two women standing close together, and her lip curled.

"It's so nice to see such supportiveness behind the scenes," she purred. Lisa waited for the sting behind the smile, and it soon came. "Of course, you can afford to be friendly when you know you're not in the running for the serious competition."

Lisa drew in a sharp breath, but before she'd found the words to speak, she remembered Redmond's admonition. A catfight would just make them both look foolish and unprofessional.

Instead, she met Caroline's gaze and rolled her eyes, and Caroline grinned back. They both knew it was fear and insecurity that fuelled Tiffany's bitchiness.

"Time we were getting on," Lisa said, wanting to put distance between herself and Tiffany, who was still fiddling with her acrylic nails.

Once they were on set, there was little Tiffany could say, but as Lisa and Caroline left the room, she fired off one parting shot.

"See you afterwards. Well, Lisa anyway. I imagine you'll survive until next week. Caroline, it's been nice to see you again."

"Bitch," Lisa couldn't help murmuring under her breath, counting on the creak of the door closing to cover the sound to all except Caroline.

"Ignore her," Caroline said calmly. "It's true, anyway. We were far the weakest dancers last week, we'll be first off. But it doesn't matter. Being here was an experience, and it's publicity for the studio. We're doing OK anyway, and we don't need this, not really. It's different for people like you and Red. You were made to be stars."

"He was," Lisa agreed. She'd never felt the same herself. In Redmond's absence, she'd become one weak meteor in a falling shower, and even though his arrival had set her back on high, she wasn't wholly convinced it would last.

"Oh, you two were made for each other." Caroline smiled. "If you can't see it, you're the only one. But I thought now you were going out, you'd have to believe it."

The temptation to tell the truth was almost overwhelming, but she bit it back. She was so tired of lying to all her friends outside the dancing world. It was some consolation that Jerry knew how things had begun with Red, and didn't judge her for it, but she had no confidence that Terri or Marian would share that attitude, and while Caroline was clearly sympathetic, Lisa certainly couldn't tell the truth to someone so closely connected with the show. So she contented herself with remarking, "I'm not quite used to it yet, I guess. It still seems a bit too good to be true. Not that I'm complaining."

Then they were at the door of the studio, and there was no more chance to talk, as they were bustled in and settled on the sofa. Most of the men were already arranged in a line on the other sofa, and Harry was the last to join them, a moment before Phillipa came in and the cameras started rolling.

Lisa didn't take in much of the preliminary chat, in which Phillipa reminded the audience of the rules. The time seemed to fly by until she reached, "The couple judged weakest by the judges, and therefore the first couple to be leaving the show is..." Then there was what seemed an interminable pause and Lisa met Redmond's eyes across the room. Even though she agreed with Tiffany and Caroline's assessment, there was still a flutter of fear and doubt inside her. What if she was wrong? What if the collision had counted against her more than she'd thought?

Of course, that could work the other way too. If the judges had seen Tiffany's vicious action and her haste to remove herself from the scene, they might just count it against her and Harry instead. Lisa smiled. She could dream. Tiffany and Harry made for such good television, there was no way they'd be going home in the first week.

Finally the pause was at an end and Phillipa opened her mouth and took a breath.

"David and Caroline."

Even though it surprised nobody, Caroline's friendly nature would be much missed, and there was an air of sadness as the girls huddled around her, hugging her and expressing their sympathies.

Then Phillipa called Caroline and David to the microphone to say their farewells. By the end of their dignified little speech, Lisa had a lump in her throat. Since her shock with the job, her emotions seemed to have come right to the surface, and she tried to force them away. As Phillipa called the remaining couples to the floor for a jive, there could be no room in her mind for anything but Redmond and the dance.

Standing on the floor and waiting as Phillipa introduced the band and babbled away about the choice of song, Lisa felt edgy and restless, as she always had during the long waits at competitions when waiting for the last dancer to answer to their called number. And why was it, Lisa wondered, that it was always the men who went missing, leaving their partners standing alone on the dance floor looking lost and embarrassed, and pathetically relieved when the missing men strolled in looking perfectly happy and relaxed? Lisa had been in that situation a few times, and she was relieved that this time Redmond was here beside her, flashing her his vivid grin as Phillipa finally stopped talking and the conductor raised his arms to tell the band to strike up their intro.

When the first notes of her favourite jive rang out, Lisa didn't have to make an effort to smile for the cameras. The music ran right through her, instantly lifting her mood and setting her feet dancing of their own accord. Redmond seemed to sense her delight and smiled back at her as he led her through the agreed routine, but took advantage of a moment when they drew closer together to mouth something which Lisa thought might be "feeling brave?"

She nodded, wondering what she'd let herself in for, but feeling certain that in this light mood, with their perfect connection, she could follow it. So she let Redmond lead her into a deep drop, swinging her dangerously floorwards and up again. It felt like being on a rollercoaster—heady and exciting and a little frightening in a "let's do that again!" sort of way. She grinned brilliantly up at Redmond, who gave her an approving nod and smile.

As the music died, Redmond spun her in towards him and ended by wrapping her in a tight embrace and lowering his lips to hers. For a moment she forgot the room full of crowds and cameras, and when she started noticing it again, there was ringing applause and raised voices calling out in support of their favourites. She thought they were getting quite a bit of support, but just now it didn't seem to matter so much anyway whether they won. It was enough to have danced the way they had.

Dizzy with delight and relief, Lisa hung on Redmond's arm as he escorted her back to the sofa. This time, without waiting for permission from the presenters, the dancers sat down in their couples and watched as the screens replayed snippets from the dancing, accompanied by comments from the judges.

"No competition," Red whispered, not very discreetly.

"Shhh," Lisa hissed, but she couldn't help smiling at his confidence. She didn't entirely share it, but she had to admit there were only a few serious contenders, so she and Red should certainly make it through this week.

Would that make it all worth it? she wondered. Would being in the final—or even winning—make up for the shock of losing her job, the fear and uncertainty? She was surprised to find that now she'd relaxed a little, she faced the prospect of looking for something new to do with something less like fear and more like... excitement. Perhaps it was time for a change. She looked around the room, drinking in the buzz of excitement, the colours, the sparkle. No doubt about it: the dull greys of the office paled in comparison. This was where she wanted to be.

And now she would have a whole week to wait, to find out whether they would stay to dance another week. Oh, she knew they deserved to go through all right, but that meant nothing until you heard the judges' verdict. Judges, after all, were human. They could be wrong, catch you at the wrong moment, be stupid or unobservant or just plain prejudiced. You weren't safe until your number was called. That was the mantra she'd grown up with, and it had always kept her on tenterhooks as the floor filled up with dancers.

When the judges complimented their performance, especially the dramatic drop, Lisa felt less excitement than relief. Redmond flung his arms around her shoulders and squeezed and kissed her as if he felt elated, though she wasn't sure whether it was just a performance for the cameras. That was the trouble with being a performer. You learnt to hide your emotions, and then you learnt to distrust the emotions you saw in others. She knew she had a wide, delighted smile to match his, even though her stomach was already starting to clench at the thought of how much more difficult the next week's dancing might be.

What was Redmond thinking?

Looking closely, she thought she could detect a hint of tension in his jaw, a distance in his eyes. As the judges went on with their reports, Redmond seemed to be only half listening to them. His eyes were focused elsewhere, waiting for something.

Phillipa asked a few of the couples for their thoughts, but Lisa and Red were not among them. Lisa, who'd long since learned to pick out the important information and discard the rest, paid no attention to Tiffany's half sweet, half barbed, remarks. She was busy wondering whether she was right about Redmond's preoccupation, and if so, what was so fascinating to him. When Phillipa remarked that they were coming to the end of the evening's show, Redmond seemed to become a little more alert. Lisa took her cue from him and listened as the blonde intoned, "We're hoping that one of tonight's couples will have something extra special to celebrate. One very lucky lady's partner would like to make her evening. You know who you are, so come on out."

Phillipa was using a roving mike, and the spotlight followed her lithe figure as she strolled into the middle of the floor and held out the microphone. Beside Lisa, there was a blur of movement. She turned her head just in time to see Redmond disappearing out of his seat, bounding with his usual lithe grace into the pool of light. Phillipa faded back out as Redmond cleared his throat and began, with uncharacteristic hesitance.

"Thanks for giving me the opportunity to say something very important to my wonderful partner. Lisa, would you come up here too, please?"

Lisa almost felt as if she was watching herself from outside as she stepped onto the dance floor, her feet carrying her in their usual graceful glide while her brain drifted aimlessly. On top of all the day's strangeness, this was just too much. She didn't quite dare to think what Redmond had in store for her.

"Lisa, you've always been my perfect dancing partner, but these past few weeks have finally convinced me of what I should always have known: you're also my perfect partner in every other sense. I hope you don't mind me picking such a public occasion to say this, but I wanted everyone to know how much you mean to me, and this seemed like the perfect opportunity to ask you. Lisa…" He paused and Lisa watched numbly as he stepped closer and dropped to one knee. The spotlight trailed after him, and as it settled on him, Lisa finally, belatedly, realised what was going on. He cleared his throat and put the question she'd always dreamed he'd ask and never for a moment believed he would: "Will you marry me?"

Time seemed to slow, the roomful of people faded to a blur, music and voices became one unnoticed murmur. All her attention was focused on Redmond's eyes, looking imploringly up at her from the pool of light. Slowly, as the reality of his words sank in, her mouth curved into a beaming smile. She desperately wanted to say yes, but somehow her voice was sticking in her throat, and so she nodded, once, slowly. It was enough. In a moment, Redmond was on his feet, embracing her. The room came back to life and Lisa hid her head against Redmond's shoulder to shut out the sea of faces, but the waves of applause and laughter and shouting still beat against her ears.

All too soon, their embrace was cut short by Phillipa taking back her microphone and hustling Redmond and Lisa off the floor.

They were immediately surrounded by people slapping them on the back and offering congratulations. Most of them were people Lisa hardly knew, and she wondered whether Redmond did either. She was relieved to see Mark and Elaine shouldering their way through the crowd at the edge of the dance floor.

Elaine fussed delightedly over Lisa while Mark and Redmond made a path through the crowd for them.

"My lovely fiancée and I would like some time together." Redmond smiled charmingly at everyone who tried to detain them, and soon they were on their way out of the studio. Today nobody would hassle them to return their costumes immediately or sign out of the building. Even to the officious Barbie doll receptionists, some things were sacred.

Chapter 13

Lisa breathed a huge sigh of relief when the door of Redmond's flat closed behind them, but it was followed immediately by a wave of awkwardness. What happened now? It was all very well for Redmond to go down on his knees in front of a roomful of people, and for her to nod helplessly because she could never refuse him anything, but she had no idea what it was that she'd agreed to. They'd never had a chance to discuss marriage. A big wedding or a small family occasion, in church or a registry office… Would they even set a wedding date, or did he just mean the question in an abstract "let's get engaged" sort of way? She couldn't imagine where they went from here.

Redmond took her hand and pulled her onto the bed beside him, and she nestled into his arms. That way the world felt a little less frightening. Suddenly she realised how tired she was after all the day's excitement. No wonder everything felt so bizarre and unreal. She'd never had a day like this in her life… it had started with losing her job and things had only become weirder since then.

"Did we really just get engaged?" she murmured drowsily into Redmond's shirt.

"Uh huh." The amused tone was back and she wished she hadn't said something quite so idiotic.

In an attempt to redeem herself by making her daft remark sound like the prelude to a more sensible question, she tacked on, "So now what?"

She meant about rings and announcements and weddings, but, whether deliberately or otherwise, he misinterpreted her question and answered, "Now we get some sleep and then tomorrow we go to see Mark and Elaine, and practice some more."

Well, it answered the question as far as it went, she supposed. Of course Mark and Elaine, the nearest thing she had in the world to family, would want to talk to them properly after their hasty exit from the ballroom. And maybe, just maybe, their presence would unlock Redmond's tongue a little, because he certainly didn't seem forthcoming tonight.

"OK?" Red asked as he lazily began undressing her.

"That wasn't what I meant," Lisa answered, pulling away from him and going to grab her nightdress. Any other time she would have welcomed his enthusiasm. Considering they'd just got engaged, it was ridiculous to be avoiding him, and if it had been a normal engagement she wouldn't have been, but she still wasn't entirely sure she trusted his sudden devotion, and she could do with some space to get her head round the change.

"What did you mean?" Red sat up, realising that things weren't going the way he'd had in mind.

"I meant, what happens about us." Just the word 'us' tripped her up. She wasn't used to there being an 'us.'

"In what way?" Red wasn't making this easy for her.

"What are we going to do when we get married?" She didn't let herself use the word 'if', although it had crossed her mind. She had to start believing Red meant what he said. "Are we going to live here? In America? What am I going to do for work?"

"Whatever you like," Red said lazily, as if they were just agreeing on a restaurant for Sunday lunch. "We've got loads of time to plan. Can't we just enjoy being together for now, and get through the competition? It's only a few weeks."

"Only a few weeks, and then what? How can you just go along without knowing what's around the corner?"

Red laughed, then, and stood up and gathered her into an embrace. "It's always worked for me, but I'm sorry. I know you're a planner, and I guess I'll have to get used to that, but really, do you need to sort it all right now? Can't we get some sleep first?" He pulled her down onto the bed and nibbled playfully at her neck.

"Sleep?" she queried.

"Maybe not," he grinned, tugging her nightie from her hand and throwing it aside.

"Not sleeping could be good," Lisa conceded, deciding to set aside her worries at least until the morning.

*

After that, they settled comfortably into a temporary routine of long hours of practice followed by evenings of teaching. Red continued to insist that he was happy to stay in London if it was what Lisa wanted, and she almost believed him, although it had crossed her mind that even if he believed it himself, his feelings might still change, especially if they didn't win the competition. So she threw herself into dancing, and consigned her job hunt to spare moments.

Somehow she did find time to get the corner shop to order in *Marketing Week* for her, but the job ads never seemed to contain anything quite right. The positions were either too senior, or too junior, or in fields outside her experience. And when one turned up which she could have done, it turned out to be away from London, and there was no point in applying for jobs elsewhere until after the show at least. In the end she signed up with a few temping agencies and postponed the problem of her real career until after the show. As Redmond had said, if they won, or even made the final, there was a good chance of a career in dance, and then she wouldn't have to worry about dull campaigns ever again.

The agencies still hadn't rung her by the end of that week, and she was guiltily glad to go into the next round without new-job nerves hanging over her.

Lisa and Redmond heard nothing from the film crews all week, but the buzz in the papers and on the Internet was still that they were serious contenders. By the time they arrived at the studio on Saturday, Lisa was settling in there, but she knew she mustn't allow herself to become complacent. All the couples were stunning and the waltz was Xander and Kasia's best dance, so there was serious competition.

Still, Lisa knew she looked and felt good in the dress she'd been given, a stunning confection of icing-sugar white and mint coloured froth. And she still remembered the magic of the waltz she and Redmond had danced the first day they got together after his return from the States. She knew they'd do well if she could let go of the thought of the audience and the other competitors, and just float away on the music, guided gently by Redmond's strong arms.

As long as they went through. This time, there was much less agreement on who was likely to be sent home. Al and Eveline were perhaps less polished and experienced dancers than some of the others, but Fritz and Kathrin were better at ballroom than Latin, and jive wasn't their favourite dance. Harry and Tiffany had danced well but not spectacularly, and although Lisa thought her and Redmond's performance had been one of the best, she thought that at least one of the judges might disapprove of their non-traditional style.

There was simply no way of knowing how the results would turn out this week, and because of that, all the dancers held their breath when the moment finally arrived for Phillipa to pause and make a show of opening the envelope which contained the judges' vote.

"Al and Eveline," Phillipa announced finally, and there was a collective rush of breath. Al and Eveline looked stunned at the result, and Fritz and Kathrin equally so. Then, after the usual round of hugging and comments, but before Lisa had quite stopped shaking with relief, it was finally time to dance.

As usual, Lisa's limbs had stiffened as she sat on the sofa, and she stretched surreptitiously as she rose. Out of the corner of her eye, she could see Redmond doing the same, and she remembered how he reached out, loosening his long limbs, as he emerged from bed in the mornings. Really, she thought, she'd been so busy worrying about work and the show, she hadn't been appreciating her time with him half enough. She'd have to see what she could do about that.

In the meantime, the remaining four couples were settling themselves into their spaces on the floor, keeping by unspoken mutual consent to different corners so that there was less chance of collision.

With only four couples, it was easier than before to set aside thoughts as to what the others were doing, and just dance as if nothing mattered except Lisa, Redmond, and the slow dreamy music that could have been made for them. They floated their way round three sides of the floor but when they came to the fourth side and a slow heel turn, Lisa felt something give underneath her, and she suddenly felt as if she was dancing on sponge. A step later, when she moved forward on her heel, she realised what was wrong. The heel of her shoe had given way, and as she stepped onto it, she lurched uncomfortably and just managed to save herself from falling. Thanking her lucky stars that they were near the end of the routine, she finished it on her toes with the loose heel dragging awkwardly, sometimes behind and sometimes underneath her straining foot.

As soon as she sat down on the sofa and made to unbuckle her broken shoe, she found Phillipa standing over her with the microphone.

"It looks as if we'll have to call you unlucky Lisa from now on! First the crash in week one, and then I saw you slip out there. What happened?"

In answer, Lisa held up the shoe she'd just removed, with the heel dangling pathetically from the upper.

"Bad luck," she agreed with Phillipa, "but these things happen. Let's just hope troubles don't come in threes."

"Indeed," Phillipa said, and moved on to talk to the other couples.

Lisa barely heard a word they said. She was too busy worrying how an almost brand-new shoe had broken on her. Bad luck? Maybe. But with Tiffany sharing a dressing room, she wouldn't be surprised if it had had help. From now on, she wasn't letting her shoes out of her sight once Tiffany was in the building.

*

"That was bad luck," Redmond remarked as they were leaving, heading for Lisa's flat this time. She was beginning to wonder why they bothered maintaining two separate flats, considering that they were never apart all week, just took turns moving from one to the other.

"Yeah," Lisa agreed. She wasn't going to say anything about her suspicions, just to have Redmond tell her off for making unfounded accusations. Close though they were, she knew he wasn't wholly on her side. And he still kept disappearing during the evenings to make phone calls to America that he wouldn't explain. Once she'd been so paranoid, she'd even tried to ask Elaine, who'd immediately looked shifty and evasive. But surely Elaine wouldn't collude in anything that would hurt Lisa, so there couldn't be any truth to the fantasies in Lisa's mind of Redmond whispering sweet nothings to an American girl he couldn't wait to get back home to. She knew she was being paranoid. She knew she should stop or she'd come close to driving him to do the very thing she was afraid of.

All week, though, Lisa couldn't shake the thought that something odd was going on, and it combined with her fear that the broken heel would have damaged their standing with the judges, to make her jumpy and irritable. Redmond did his best to soothe her, but in the end he took to retreating into the lounge after practices to watch Sky Sports while Lisa surfed the Internet on her laptop in the bedroom and made a vague attempt to job hunt.

All in all, it was a relief when Saturday came around again. This week it was time to rumba, and Lisa found a fabulous off-the-shoulder lilac dress with a diagonal hemmed skirt made from layers of lavender silk. It was perfect. She couldn't wait to dance in it. But first, they had to sit through Phillipa's exhaustingly polite babble. She introduced the band. She introduced the judges. And then she said something that made Lisa and all the other dancers sit up and take note.

"Although it turns out," Phillipa went on, her normally vacuous face becoming serious, "we could have given our judges a holiday for the first part of today's show, because it's already been decided who's going home today."

The couples looked at each other. This was a change to the rules, and a change they hadn't been warned about. Fritz frowned, his German precision upset by the disruption to expectations. Harry raised his eyebrows, clearly intrigued, while Tiffany smiled, confident that she was safe from whatever was about to be unleashed.

"Yes, it turns out that one of our couples has flouted the rules to be here, and so they'll be leaving the show. Regardless of the quality of their dancing, there's no place for cheats here on *Couples*. One of our couples is not a couple, and so they'll be going home."

Phillipa was clearly stringing out the suspense, and as she spoke, Lisa's heart thumped so hard she could almost feel it in her throat. Redmond looked unconcerned, and Lisa forced herself to remain calm, at least on the outside. They'd lived as a couple for weeks now, and at least most of the time it felt real. Redmond said they had a future, and she wanted to believe him. It would be too cruelly ironic if they had to leave now, because of a deception, which had in any case only lasted for the first week of the competition. And how would anyone have found out?

Of course it wouldn't surprise Lisa if Tiffany had "accidentally" let Tim know that she thought someone was cheating, but Lisa and Redmond had very little to do with her, and there was nothing she could have known that would jeopardise their position. Was there?

Phillipa was still talking, and she still hadn't mentioned a name. She explained how disappointed that the producers were to lose some great dancers so early in the series, and Lisa had never hoped more that a compliment wasn't intended to apply for her. Her fingers had tensed themselves around the folds of her skirt, and she forced them to relax, wishing that Redmond was sitting next to her so that she could twine her fingers into his for comfort. Then, finally, Phillipa said, "Take a look at this," and cued up the big screen.

The film began with a long shot of the six couples on the floor the first week, which told them nothing. Lisa could feel the tension around her. Was it possible that more than one couple believed they might be excluded?

And then, in the split second that the well-lit dance floor was replaced by a low-lit, packed nightclub dance floor, with strobe lights and dry ice smoke adding to the seedy atmosphere, Lisa realised who'd been rumbled, and her heart ached for Fritz and Kathrin, and for Jerry, who might now get his chance with Fritz, but not in the way he'd hoped.

She cringed inside for Fritz, who was sitting watching impassively as he was confronted by two almost life-size images of him draped against an attractive blond guy, dancing to an unheard beat in a way that was quite unmistakably the prelude to greater intimacy.

Seeing that Fritz was handling the situation well, Lisa turned her attention to Kathrin. Would this be a surprise to her?

At the end of the sofa, Kathrin was wide-eyed, her hand to her mouth, in an expression of shocked bewilderment just a little too stereotypical to be convincing. She'd known, then. That made things better, Lisa thought. She wasn't going to feel betrayed, except by whoever had discovered their secret and let it out.

On the screen was a grainy photograph of two blond men, presumably Fritz and the one from the nightclub, entwined.

"It could be anyone," Kathrin protested feebly over the throbbing beat of the soundtrack, but Fritz turned to her and said, gently, "It's me. I'm sorry. I can't lie anymore."

Kathrin stared for a moment, then sank her head in her hands, and when she raised it again, it was to stand and say in a slow, surprised way, "We'll be leaving then."

And then, as if released from a spell, the dancers were on their feet, crowding around Kathrin. Breaking with tradition, the men came over from their sofa to join the girls in butterfly dresses fluttering around Kathrin as if around a flower.

Lisa hesitated for a moment, then walked the other way. She could talk to Kathrin later, and Fritz had been left standing alone and lost by the other sofa.

She didn't exactly know what to say, but she knew she needed to be there. Then she wondered if she'd have felt the same if it hadn't been for the conversation she'd had with Jerry.

Still, for whatever reason, at least she was there smiling nervously at Fritz as he spoke, so softly she could hardly hear him. "I feel bad. For Kathrin. And my family."

"They don't know?"

He shook his head and Lisa winced. What a way to find out. But at least he wouldn't have to lie anymore. It was too late for that. She hoped he'd soon find out that he had at least one sincere admirer. Over Fritz's shoulder, she could see Jerry fidgeting in the middle of the second row of seats, clearly anxious to get closer to the object of his devotions.

"I'm sure it'll be OK. I hope it will," Lisa said.

"Thank you," Fritz said, and he smiled at her, a weak brave smile that melted her heart and showed her what Jerry found so appealing. Then Fritz turned away and walked slowly off the stage, and as she returned to her seat, Lisa could see Jerry muttering and excusing his way out of his seat.

Kathrin too had gone, and Phillipa waited until most of the dancers were back in their seats before resorting to theatrical cliché. "Well, that was a surprise development, but the show must go on, and now it's time for our remaining three couples to go head to head in the world's most romantic dance. A rumba."

The couples took to the floor and took their starting positions. Lisa, leaning away from Redmond yet holding herself in perfect balance with him, was able to look around the floor and see Tiffany, looking like an ice maiden in pale blue with silver frosting, turn her back on Harry and strike a pose of disinterest. Lisa couldn't remember where she'd seen this routine before, but it was definitely familiar. Any moment now, when the music started, Harry would sidle up to her and turn her towards him, only to be rebuffed. Then the two of them would enter into an intricate sequence of advances and retreats.

At the far end of the floor, Xander and Kasia were crouched low, ready to rise with the music like flowers blooming from the ground. For once, Lisa felt, she and Redmond were being conventional. But hopefully they wouldn't need gimmicks to make their rumba memorable. The slow, dreamy Latin beat gave time for plenty of expression, and in practice she and Red had been dancing a sizzling rumba. Now she just needed the music to start up before her arm began to ache too much.

Locking eyes with Redmond, she realised he was thinking the same thing. Then the first note came, and even before the beat had come in, Red was leading her into their first slow walks. He promenaded her proudly closer to the centre of the floor, then turned her this way and that, using slow caressing movements that would have seduced her in seconds if that hadn't already happened.

After the awkwardness of the previous week and her broken shoe, it was a relief to find that everything flowed smoothly for her and Redmond, and as the music came to an end and she relaxed against him, she could feel a smile spreading across her face. She'd been looking forward to the relief of having completed a good dance without any shoe disasters or crashes, but now that it was over, she wished she could start all over again.

*

"I was so nervous," she told Redmond in the car home, almost babbling with relief.

"Why? Your rumba's amazing. Or were you just worried about your shoes?" Red joked.

"Well, yes, I was a bit worried about my shoes. But I was more worried when they said about having found out that someone was cheating. I thought we were going to get kicked out then."

"Why? We're not cheating. Come on, pretending we got together a bit sooner than we did is hardly the same as pretending to be with a woman when you're gay. Now, that was a surprise."

Now it was Lisa's turn to act knowing. "Come on, it can't have been that much of a surprise. It's pretty obvious Fritz is that way inclined." Although she might not have known if Jerry hadn't pointed it out.

"You never said anything."

"Well, no. Fritz's love life is none of my business."

"But the show is." Redmond took in a sharp breath, as if something had just occurred to him. "It wasn't you who told them, was it?"

Lisa was shocked. "Of course not! I didn't know, only suspected. And if I had known, I wouldn't have said. We're hardly in any position to enforce the rules."

"But nobody knows that," Red pointed out. Lisa hoped he didn't mean it. "You're not very competitive, are you?" he went on.

"Yes, I am. I want nothing more than to win… fair and square, not by knocking the competition."

Red laughed and shook his head, but he didn't argue. After a moment, he said, "Talking of the competition, it's getting tougher. I hope you're still feeling confident."

Lisa didn't quite know what to say to that.

"I think we've got as good a chance as anyone," she said eventually.

"Better," Redmond amended.

"Maybe. I don't know. Xander and Kasia are good."

"True. But it's tango next time. Do you remember Xander at the Nationals before Kasia got pregnant?"

She did. He'd looked like Arnold Schwarzenegger in tails, trying to dominate the dance floor.

"I think he's improved since then, but you're right, tango's not his dance. If Tiffany and Harry stay in, that could be tougher. Tango suits them better."

"Not really. They're sharp, I'll give them that. But too icy. Tango needs fire. She should be a dragon, and she always looks as if she's swallowed a packet of frozen peas."

Lisa laughed, as she was no doubt intended to.

All the same, the competition next weekend was going to be tough, and they'd have to focus hard and prepare well over the next six days. And, just to make things more challenging, Tim had just told the three remaining couples that the last round would take place not at the TV studios where they'd got used to filming, but in Blackpool, home of British ballroom dance and the vast, beautiful Tower Ballroom.

*

"Blackpool?" Even down the phone, Jerry's voice was excited. "Fantastic. I'll be there. Bet you can't wait!"

"I don't know. I'm excited. And scared." Lisa scrunched herself tighter into the corner of Red's huge sofa. It still felt weird being in his flat without him, but he'd popped out to do some errands and she'd decided to take the opportunity to catch up with Jerry. He'd texted to congratulate her on her engagement, but she still felt guilty that he—and so many other people—had found out from the TV rather than personally. The fact that she hadn't known in advance herself didn't seem to excuse her, although it probably should have done.

"It'll be fine. You two are burning up the floor."

"I know." Lisa also knew how dubious her voice sounded. She wasn't only scared of losing. She was also nervous about the competition coming to an end. As long as she and Red were still dancing, she knew where she was. After that, all the questions that they'd agreed to postpone until after the final show would come rushing in.

"Everything is all right between you, isn't it?" Jerry asked. His uncanny ability to pick up what was going on in her head no longer surprised her.

"Ye-e-es." The slowness of Lisa's answer told its own story, and she knew she'd have to expand, or have the answer dragged out of her. "Except that... I don't know... it's hard really to believe in a wedding or a future when all Red ever wants to talk about is tomorrow. It's like everything after the competition is a big void."

Jerry laughed. "Don't worry about it, darling, it's a guy thing. Plans are for the girls. Redmond's always been a day-by-day kind of guy. It'll take him a while to change that. You can't expect him to go from flying by the seat of his pants one day to living by a ten year plan the next."

It was more or less what Red had said himself, but it didn't help as much as both Red and Jerry seemed to think it should.

"It wasn't me that asked him to change! He was the one who brought up marriage, and marriage is a forever thing. What's the point in talking about marriage if you can't think beyond tomorrow?" Lisa thumped the sofa arm in frustration.

"I know," Jerry soothed her. "But you have to admit, a lot is going to depend on the competition. If you win, you can do pretty much anything."

"And if we don't?"

"Worry about it when it happens. But it won't, because you two are amazing together. Everyone can see it. He's crazy about you, and you love him, don't you?"

"Of course I love him." Lisa wasn't sure she'd ever said it out loud, but she knew Jerry knew it just the same. "I just don't know if I can live with him."

"You'll learn. Give it time."

"I guess." Lisa wasn't convinced but if she carried on she'd just end up arguing around in circles.

"Seriously. You'll be great. I can't wait to dance at your wedding. But first I'll be watching you two win at Blackpool. And hopefully Fritz will be with me." Jerry's voice lingered on Fritz's name like a caress. Lisa wished, not for the first time, that she could fall in love as deeply and uncomplicatedly as Jerry. Although this time things didn't seem to be quite so simple.

"How are things with Fritz?" she asked, feeling guilty that it hadn't crossed her mind earlier. Her world seemed to have narrowed to the competition, and now that Fritz was out of the running, he'd slipped out of her thoughts.

"Good. Turns out his family weren't totally surprised, and he's a lot happier now it's out in the open."

"And the guy in the nightclub?" Now she knew Fritz was OK, her concern was for Jerry. For once, he seemed serious in his feelings, and she didn't want him getting his heart broken.

"Just some guy. Fritz didn't even take his number."

"So he's free and single?"

"Not for much longer," Jerry laughed. "We went out last night, and we're meeting again tomorrow after practice. Blackpool, here we come!"

"Blackpool." Lisa raised a hand in an imaginary toast, and knew that Jerry would be doing the same. "Blackpool and the show. One thing's for sure, it's certainly changing a few lives already."

Lisa heard Red's key in the door. That was one change. She couldn't believe how used she was becoming to Redmond in her life, or how her heart still leapt when he returned.

"Hi," she called, and Redmond came in, kicked off his shoes, and kissed her on the top of the head.

"Hi Red," Jerry added. "I'll leave you two lovebirds in peace, shall I?"

"OK," Lisa agreed. "See you soon."

She dropped the phone, intending to ask Redmond what he'd been doing, but when he fell onto the sofa beside her and pulled her back for a proper kiss, she decided that Red and Jerry were right. Once again, the questions could wait.

Chapter 14

Arriving at the hotel on Friday afternoon, Lisa and Redmond checked in together, and Lisa marveled that already it seemed thoroughly natural to go up to their room together, taking a moment to sneak a kiss in the lift on the way. Without discussing it, they seemed even to have come to an agreement about who would lay claim to which side of the bed. They wouldn't have trouble convincing anyone they were a couple now!

Lisa flopped back on the big, soft mattress and lay there. She was surprisingly weary considering how early in the day it was. Although she'd decided to put her concerns about the future on the back burner until after the final, they had a way of sneaking back in at night, leaving her sleeping fitfully and waking more tired than she'd gone to bed. Redmond, on the other hand, seemed full of energy, and wanted to go out and explore the town.

"Do I have to? It's so comfortable here. And Blackpool won't have changed. The same tacky arcades, the same pointless shops, the same cold wind." Lisa kicked off her shoes and curled up under the duvet to emphasise her point.

"Stay if you like. I'm going to have a look around," Redmond said, making for the door.

"Hang on—I'll come!" Lisa got little enough time to spend with Redmond—she didn't want to waste any. And besides, it wouldn't do her any good being left alone to brood.

After a brief look in some of the tackier gift shops and a laugh about the absurd items for sale, Redmond led her down to the beach. The sky was just beginning to soften to a sunset pink, and Lisa had to admit that it was beautiful, but it wasn't long before she decided she needed to get out of the chill wind. Redmond accompanied her back to the hotel, despite her insistence that he go on without her if he wanted to.

On the way back to the hotel, Redmond's mobile rang. The shrill sound no longer startled Lisa. She'd learned to recognise it, and hate it for the way it could always interrupt their lives and their time together.

Redmond greeted the caller, listened for a moment, and said, "OK. I'm with someone at the moment. Can I call you back shortly?"

Lisa laughed at his crisp, professional tones. If she'd been on the other end of the phone, she'd have pictured him in a suit at a big mahogany desk, talking to a couple of Wall Street power brokers, not strolling through Blackpool with a recently unemployed would-be dance professional.

"You could have taken the call," she said when he hung up. "I don't mind."

"I'd rather talk to you," Redmond said. "Anyway, it's kind of confidential at the moment, and even if it wasn't it's better that I don't tell you too much about what might be happening until it's a bit more definite."

Now Lisa's curiosity was piqued, and they squabbled gently about it all the way back to the hotel.

Then Redmond vanished into a borrowed meeting room with his mobile phone. She still hadn't got a word out of him about what was going on. It annoyed her. She told him everything that was happening in her life. He'd even been the first to know about her job situation. And in return, she got precisely nothing.

She was delighted to run into Elaine in the lobby, which gave her a chance to grumble, but Elaine just laughed at her.

"What do you expect?" Elaine said. "It's Redmond. He'll tell you when he's good and ready."

And with that Lisa had to be content, because Elaine instantly drew her over to a table and started a discussion about the dancing and dresses in the previous round, and what Lisa and Redmond would be wearing for the all-important final.

"No idea." Lisa shrugged.

Elaine was scandalised, but Lisa laughingly threw her own words back at her: "What do you expect? It's Redmond. Well, Redmond and the wardrobe department. I just turn up and do what I'm told."

"That's a first," Elaine teased. "So, how's life apart from Redmond and dancing?"

"Lousy," Lisa shot back with unusual vehemence, causing Elaine to raise her eyebrows and Mark, who'd just approached the table with a tray, to flinch dramatically and pretend to change his mind and retreat to a free table with the two coffees he'd just collected from the bar.

"Why?" Elaine asked, grabbing Mark's wrist to prevent him fleeing, and narrowly avoiding pitching both the drinks to the floor.

So Lisa briefly recounted the story of her disaster. Elaine rolled her eyes at Lisa's stupidity, while Mark, surprisingly, was sympathetic.

Both of them made reassuring noises that "something will turn up," which she found unreasonably annoying. What did they know about employment outside the dancing world? It was years since they'd done anything except run the studio, and it wasn't as if they had any concrete suggestions, just kind, encouraging mumblings that meant nothing in the end.

"Everyone's so bloody sure that it'll all sort itself out—you'd think worrying had been banned," she grumbled to Redmond afterwards, when he finished his call and came to escort her up to their room.

"So it should be, with the final coming up. Plenty of time to worry afterwards if you find you need to. But you can't let it spoil the competition. A job is just a job. Dancing is your life. Don't tell me that's not true—you couldn't dance the way you do if you didn't care so much about it."

"Caring doesn't pay the bills, though."

"No, but dancing could. Have you ever thought about teaching full time?"

"I'd love to, but I can't see it happening."

"Never say never." Redmond was his usual optimistic self, but Lisa knew just how likely it was. Mind you, Elaine had said something similar. She was almost beginning to feel that everyone else knew something she didn't. Either that, or they were pretending to, in the hope of stopping her worrying and spoiling their chances in the competition. Elaine and Mark did have a lot riding on this event, after all. It would be understandable if they were more concerned about her performance than her job. In fact, it occurred to her now, they were actually surprisingly laid back, considering the circumstances. The more she thought about it, the odder everyone's behaviour seemed.

She was about to remark on it to Redmond but they both began speaking at the same time and on balance she was more interested in hearing what he had to say.

"Go on," she insisted.

"I was just going to ask if you wanted a quick run-through of the routine before tomorrow."

"We can't get into the ballroom until tomorrow, can we?"

"No, but the hotel's got a ballroom upstairs that's not being used for a function tonight, so they've kindly agreed that we can use it, as long as we don't mind if a few of the staff come and have a look in when they're off duty."

"OK," Lisa agreed, thinking that dancing was the only thing that could take her mind off the impossibility of her situation right now. "If we're going to have an audience, should we dress for it?"

"I thought so."

Lisa laid the white dress out on the bed and eyed it critically. The stain wasn't too obvious, she thought, smiling at the memory of how it had arrived there. She looked sidelong at Redmond, wondering if he was thinking the same thing, but he was apparently absorbed in setting out his own clothes.

He must have been watching more than Lisa realised, though, because as soon as she began undressing he materialised behind her, helping to tug her T-shirt over her head and unfasten her bra.

"Shouldn't you be getting ready yourself?" Lisa felt compelled to ask.

"I've only got to change my shirt and waistcoat," he pointed out, running his thumbs down her shoulder blades and beginning massaging in soothing circles back up towards her shoulders. Lisa surrendered, leaning slightly into his hands and enjoying the way the tension dropped out of her muscles.

"You want to be careful," she murmured, "or I'll be too relaxed to dance."

"Don't worry," Redmond answered, and Lisa was sure she could hear a cheeky grin in his voice. "I'm sure we can find a way of stirring you up again if necessary."

"Maybe later," she said, too drowsy to ask what he meant, although she had a suspicion she could guess. Just now she was enjoying the massage too much to care, and she was disappointed when Redmond finally dropped a kiss on her shoulder, reached for her dress, and lifted it over her head.

"Mmm, that was nice," Lisa said lazily as she smoothed down the skirt and tugged the neck straps into place. "Tie this for me?" she asked, and Redmond obliged, then turned her around and straightened the top for her, spending a little longer smoothing the fabric over her breasts than necessary.

"Ooops." He smiled, noticing how the thin fabric showed her reacting to his touch. "Better not do that if anyone's looking!"

"I should hope you weren't going to anyway," Lisa snapped back, though the snapping was largely for show. Apparently

Redmond knew what he was doing, because she felt more relaxed, yet alert, than she had all week.

"Now are you going to get ready?" she demanded.

"If I must."

"I've only got my makeup to do," Lisa pointed out.

"Okay, okay, I'm getting ready. See?" He pointedly unbuttoned his shirt.

"Good," Lisa said, in the tone she used for her kids' class when they were having an awkward day, and went to get her makeup bag.

By now, doing stage makeup was a well-practised routine that took only a few moments, so by the time Redmond was changed she was putting her brushes back in her bag and scraping her hair into a bun.

So they made their way up the sweeping staircase to the ballroom with their small CD player. Although the sound was slightly lost in the large room Lisa was soon able to lose herself in the music and Redmond's flawless leading. Her nerves and tiredness after the journey were taking their toll, however, and she was conscious that she wasn't dancing quite as well as usual. Redmond didn't say anything while they were dancing, but he frowned a lot, which added to Lisa's unease. It was a useful session, however. There were occasional interruptions from the staff, who seemed surprisingly star-struck for a hotel where Lisa would have imagined that many celebrities stayed. But in between the interruptions, Lisa and Red smoothed out their routine for the tango until they were confident with it, and still finished in plenty of time to get an early night.

*

Some time during the night she must have moved, because in the morning she woke to find herself rolled tightly in the duvet, and Redmond nowhere to be seen. A great start to their most important day so far, she thought bitterly, getting up and dragging on some tracksuit bottoms and a shirt so that she could go and look for him.

He wasn't in the restaurant, though she knew he always liked a hearty breakfast before competitions. Lisa was always too keyed up to eat beforehand, but usually made up for it afterwards. Nor was he in the meeting rooms, or the small shop by the hotel reception.

She was about to head outside to look for him when an image on the front of one of the tabloids caught her eye. It looked so familiar, it took her a second to work out what was different about the picture. Of course. Seen through the photographer's lens, she had a different perspective on Redmond's proposal to her. There was Redmond kneeling in front of her, looking up appealingly as he had when he proposed, but now she could also see her own stunned smile. Both the joy and the fear that she'd hardly dared to acknowledge to herself were clearly visible, and she shuddered at the knowledge that soon everyone would see them. Of course, the purpose of publicity was to be seen, but looking at this picture, she felt more than visible. She felt exposed.

She'd been in the papers before, of course. She and Jerry had been something of a local celebrity couple for a short while. But never anything like this. Three out of the four main tabloids had splashed one or more of the dancing couples across their front pages, and even one of the broadsheets had a postage stamp sized picture of Redmond and Lisa in one corner, this time snapped just after the proposal.

Suddenly she felt conspicuous, and wished she'd made the effort to put on some decent clothes, but curiously the scruffy outfit seemed to render her invisible. Tim was standing with his back to her, bending over a copy of the *Telegraph*, but the man he was chatting to was facing Lisa, yet was apparently oblivious to her presence.

"…sweet," the older man was saying, but Tim shook his head vehemently.

"You're kidding, right?" Tim said, and eyeing him over the random women's magazine she'd picked up, Lisa saw him shake his head vehemently. "You can't be that naïve! He knew exactly what he was doing. Has to have done." Tim waved his paper for emphasis, and the little newsprint Redmond and Lisa bobbed their heads in unison. "Win or lose, he's won in terms of publicity now, and let's face it, publicity's half the battle in this business. Maybe more than half."

Lisa's heart lurched and a sick feeling settled into the pit of her stomach.

He wouldn't have proposed to her just to ensure they were the most talked about couple in the competition. Would he? But it all stacked up so well. At first he hadn't wanted to get involved, but once he knew they had a place in the competition, he'd become so attentive she'd been fooled into thinking he cared about her, and not just about getting his face on the front of the papers. What had made her think he'd put her first, when eight years ago he'd proved that his career came before everything?

Lisa spun round (still a dancer, even in despair, she noticed dully) and stumbled blindly out of the shop and through the corridors to the hotel garden. She always thought best outdoors, and the sight of flowers usually brought her tranquility, but today all there was to look at was evergreens and the dead heads of roses killed by the first frost. The garden certainly suited her mood. Round and round she went, gathering arguments on both sides.

She picked up a last lingering daisy and tugged at the petals. Redmond had been there for her constantly since he returned to England (he loves me) but he hadn't kept in touch while he was away and for all she knew he'd leave again tomorrow (he loves me not). He'd been instantly at her side when she stumbled outside the restaurant (he loves me) but his first thought had been her dancing, not herself (he loves me not). He'd asked her to marry him (he loves me) but refused to talk about it afterwards (he loves me not). He'd proposed in front of thousands of people—but because he loved her so much, or because he wanted the audience to remember Lisa and Redmond out of all the contestants?

So he'd taken advantage of a publicity opportunity, she argued with herself—did that make him a bad person? Did it mean her answer should have been different? It wasn't as if there was anyone else she wanted. Wasn't a marriage of convenience with Redmond still a million times better than being married to anyone else? Logically she thought it would be, but her heart resisted. This wasn't what she'd waited for, what she'd dreamed of all these years. She had to find Redmond, tell him she couldn't do it. But how would she find the strength to face him after that, to dance with him, look into his eyes and smile across the dance floor. Sure, she was an actress, but there were some limits. She knew she wouldn't be able to say a word without crying, so the only answer was not to say a word.

With her emotions clamped tightly inside, she went back indoors to smarten herself up ready for the day's dancing. Despite the dull despair settling over her, she wouldn't even consider not dancing. For one thing, dancing was all she had left, and for another, Elaine and Mark's hopes for the studio were resting on her and Redmond. She couldn't let them down.

Mercifully, the room was still empty when she got back, so she quickly tugged on her dress and took a book to the far corner of the lobby to hide until it was time to dance. She didn't want to see Redmond today for longer than she needed to. Not now she'd realised what was happening. How could he? Her heart raced with anger and she pressed her fingers tightly into her palms, not minding the pain of her nails digging into her skin. It distracted her from the greater pain of realising that she'd been a fool: trusting Redmond when he told her nothing and gave away nothing except what suited him.

She found herself checking her watch every few moments, waiting for it to be time to dance. In that, at least, she knew she would find comfort. If only her partner for the day was anyone except Redmond! She'd have given anything for Jerry's cheeky grin or Gavin's clumsy efforts, but then she'd be giving up Elaine and Mark's hopes along with hers. For them, she must be strong, until after the final. Then she could flee from this terrible, impossible situation. Everything she'd ever wanted was hers—Redmond in her bed and his ring soon to be on her finger—but how could she enjoy it when she was so certain it was happening for all the wrong reasons? Maybe, she thought with a sudden flash of hope, it wasn't selfishness that motivated him, but a confused sort of kindness—wanting things to succeed for Mark and Elaine and maybe even a little for her, because if the studio took off, she'd have a job there and he could return to America knowing that she was safe and happy. That made her feel a little less gloomy, but still the thought of his departure, when she'd let herself believe for the last few ridiculous, wonderful weeks that he'd be staying, cut her to the quick.

She let her book fall to her lap and picked up a shoe brush instead. A vigorous attack on her suede soles was often the best antidote to rage and fear.

"There you are!" Redmond sounded so relieved as he flung himself into the seat beside her, she could almost have believed he'd meant every word of his dance floor declaration of love. But then, if he cared that much about winning the competition and making a go of the studio, he would be relieved that his partner hadn't run out on him. And talking of running out, where on earth had he been when she'd woken up that morning? The recollection of the empty bed and rumpled sheets fueled her indignation.

"Me? What about you? I woke up this morning and you'd completely vanished. I looked for you everywhere!"

She mentally kicked herself for the inaccuracy. Redmond wasn't one to let such intellectual laziness pass unchallenged, and sure enough he gave a slow smug smile.

"Not everywhere, or you'd have found me. I was on the phone."

"When are you ever not?" Lisa was stung. What were these conversations that so often proved more important to him than talking to her, dancing with her, or waking up with her?

"Now," Redmond pointed out calmly. Lisa had watched him deal calmly with irate shop assistants, dancers, airport baggage handlers. It had amused and impressed her, but now he turned the ability to her, she found it maddening. Was he saying that she, his fiancée of the past few weeks, was just like another annoyed staff member to be placated?

Anger bubbled just under the surface of her calmness. She wanted to shout, scream, stamp her feet. For weeks the tension had been building, with the strangeness of life with Redmond, the uncertainty of their fragile new relationship, and the precarious position she found herself in after losing her job. Now it wanted to erupt but she knew that she had to hold it in check a little longer.

"Shall we head off?" she asked, keeping her voice level, and standing immediately so that Redmond had no choice but to rise and follow her.

"Aren't we getting a cab with Elaine and Mark?" His use of the American term made him seem more distant than ever.

"Yeah, but we'd better get going soon." She checked the big brass clock above the reception desk. It was half an hour until they were officially due at the Tower for filming, but it was worth leaving some extra time for makeup and wardrobe. "Do you want to call their room and tell them we're ready?"

"A kiss for luck first?" Redmond suggested, pausing out of the way near the lifts, or as he would say, elevators. Lisa was feeling the sting of acting like his girlfriend even worse than she had at the start of the competition, but she knew she had to, at least for another day, so she obliged with a quick peck on the cheek.

As they moved on towards the phones to call Elaine, she commented that she wasn't familiar with that superstition.

"I'm not surprised," Redmond laughed. "I made it up. But you have to admit it's a good one."

Lisa punched him on the arm.

"Ow. You bully! I won't be able to dance now!"

"Rubbish."

"You're a hard-hearted woman, Lisa Darby."

But Lisa knew that wasn't true, and judging by his expression, so did he.

She was saved from replying by Elaine's appearance in the lobby, followed by Mark.

"All ready?" Elaine asked.

"Ready as we'll ever be," Lisa gave her trademark reply.

"The taxi's here," Elaine pointed out, and they all hurried outside and piled in. It was only a short distance to the ballroom, but Lisa was grateful to be out of the cold.

Once they arrived at the Tower Ballroom, Elaine and Mark were directed to seats in the gallery.

"Break a leg!" Elaine called to Redmond and Lisa over her shoulder as they headed for the stairs.

Lisa knew it was what you were meant to say, but she hated hearing it. She'd always thought how ironic it would be if, after that, someone actually fell and broke their leg. She didn't see how wishing bad things on people brought them luck.

Redmond, who knew how she felt about it, squeezed her hand as he led her through to the area reserved for performers and crew.

This was the worst part of any competition. Dancing she could handle. No matter what the pressure, she could always enjoy the experience. But waiting was horrible, and more so when so much depended on the outcome. This was their big chance, and Redmond looked infuriatingly calm. How did he do that?

Looking sideways at his expressionless face, she wondered if he was as calm as he looked. How would she know? Redmond gave nothing away unless he chose to. It was a trait she found fascinating, enviable, and infuriating.

"Aren't you nervous?" Lisa asked.

"What's the point? It doesn't make you perform any better."

"Oh!" Lisa was even more aggravated. Real nerves weren't something you could turn on and off at will, to help your performance. They just happened, and there was nothing you could do about them.

She was about to argue but then bit her tongue, realising that her irritation was at least partly caused by her nervousness. She could argue about it later, if she still cared. For now, she decided she'd better go and get ready, and then sit quietly and try, if not to relax, at least to concentrate on her performance.

On the way in, she'd seen a few familiar faces from the audience: ex-students of Elaine and Mark's, teachers and dancers she recognised from the circuit, as well as a few minor celebrities. The audience here was much bigger than the studio audience, and it was going to be daunting to see all those faces watching, and still more so to think of the thousands more people watching at home.

With one part of her mind worrying about the huge scale of the show, and another about what would happen with Redmond once the show finished, she hardly noticed the costume and makeup preparations. Even Tiffany was quiet, presumably now uncertain whether they would be one of the two couples going head to head today. Strangely, Lisa hadn't thought much during the week about the possibility of being knocked out at this stage, but it hit her now as Phillipa summoned each of the couples in turn onto the dance floor to be presented to the crowds.

As she walked out onto the dance floor, she felt as if she was stepping towards the edge of a precipice. She clung tightly to Redmond's hand as they walked on, bowed to the audience on three sides and the judges on the fourth, as protocol demanded, and then walked back to their seats to sit through the reminder of last week's dances, and the judges' opinions.

Finally the moment came. One couple wouldn't be dancing in the final. "And the couple who will be leaving at this stage of the competition…" A long pause. "…is…" An even longer pause. "…Xander and Kasia."

Redmond and Lisa stared at each other. Lisa only realised now that she'd assumed Harry and Tiffany would be the ones leaving. She wondered if Redmond had thought the same. In one way, this result was better for them. Normally Xander and Kasia were the more polished dancers, so Harry and Tiffany were less of a threat. On the other hand, Harry and Tiffany were more likely to fight dirty. Lisa remembered the first quickstep and shivered. She'd hate it if something like that happened today.

"For this final round," Phillipa went on, "the couples will be dancing individually, so once you've said your goodbyes, would Tiffany and Harry please take to the floor?"

Lisa's heart was thumping as she wished Xander and Kasia well and then returned to her seat to watch their rivals perform. They'd chosen a very traditional tune, and their routine was, Lisa thought, uninspired. Then again, maybe that was wishful thinking. The audience seemed impressed, stamping and shouting as the music ended.

Then there was no time to think anymore, as Lisa and Redmond took their positions and waited for the pounding beat of the modern tango they'd chosen to dance to.

There was a long moment of silence, during which she and Redmond faced each other with a challenging gaze that was, at least on her side, as much an expression of her real feelings as a part of the dance. Then the music began: a familiar melody dancing over a powerful throbbing beat. The words spoke to Lisa, dragging her anger, hurt and fear to the surface, so that as she approached Redmond and turned away, drew him to her only to be repulsed in her turn, her true feelings showed themselves in her gestures and expressions. She begged, pleaded, yearned, and then finally turned away, showing in every haughty line how she rejected him.

Now it was his turn to plead, with tender, eloquent gestures, until finally their fingertips touched and then, in a moment, she was in his arms, whirling and floating as lightly as a bird fluttering among the clouds. It felt perfect, and for a moment she forgot all the worries and concerns and frustrations that had been darkening her mind. In Redmond's arms, she was light and carefree and alive, spinning and dipping and loving every moment. As the music faded, they drifted apart again, and when the final beat sounded, Redmond threw himself to his knees, his eyes fixed yearningly on hers, and then as the crowd applauded, the world flooded in again.

They held the pose for long enough to allow the applause and shouting to die down a little, and then Redmond took her arm and walked her back toward her seat.

"Well, if that doesn't do it, nothing will," Redmond murmured in her ear, bringing her back to reality with a bump. Of course. It wasn't about real feelings. It was just about winning. After all the thinking she'd done on that subject in the garden, how had she let herself forget that, even for an instant? She'd danced her heart out, but Redmond had just been going through the motions. She mustn't ever forget what an extraordinary actor he was, as well as a dancer. She mustn't ever believe it was genuine. The hurt when she came back to reality was just too much.

She nodded slowly, trying to readjust her thinking, to make herself react as coolly as he did, not to thrill at the warmth of his hand laid over hers as they walked back to their seats.

Well, that was it. Now there was nothing to do but wait for the results.

The judges were talking amongst themselves, but their microphones were turned off so that the crowd and dancers had no idea of their deliberations. Redmond had kept hold of Lisa's hand and he absently played with it, stroking her fingers and caressing the sensitive skin of her palm. She willed herself not to react, either by snatching her hand away, or drawing his hand to her lips. *Do nothing. It's the safest way. Soon it will all be over and you can walk up to the podium to claim the cheque, celebrating with a kiss, or cry against Redmond's shoulder. Keep up appearances for the last time. Then you'll be free to go your way, sadder and wiser. He'll be back off to America—and there was never even a ring to return.* Although maybe she'd have kept it: a small souvenir to remind her of the few brief days when she'd thought she was loved.

"And now," Phillipa said, and an eager hush settled over the room. She deliberately kept the audience hanging on, waiting as she reminded them of the process of the competition, how the finalists had been selected, the dances they'd had to do, their different backgrounds and styles. Redmond looked calm but his hand in Lisa's had been still and tense since the presenter's speech began.

On the big screen, the compere was talking through the highlights of the filming, and then there it was: Redmond kneeling, speaking softly, and apparently sincerely as he asked for Lisa's hand in marriage. She watched numbly as the huge, wide-eyed Lisa on the screen nodded her mute acceptance, and the camera panned back to Redmond's face on which she read now a look more of relief than joy. Suddenly tears filled her eyes and one trickled down her nose and dripped onto her hand. On screen the images moved on, but Lisa couldn't let go of the image of Redmond's expression, telling her that all her fears were grounded, that his proposal was the cynical ploy she'd dreaded it might be.

She wrenched her hand from his and jumped to her feet, knowing that, no matter what was expected from her, she couldn't stay in the room with him another moment.

Redmond stood to follow her, and she forced out an excuse to keep him there.

"I don't feel great," she said shakily, and truthfully, putting her hands to her stomach to give the impression of sickness. "Probably just nerves. I'm nipping to the ladies. Back in a second."

"The results…" Redmond said, baffled, displaying yet again how little he was truly concerned for her. He didn't seem to care about her supposed illness; he just wanted her present to lend credence to their coupledom as the results were announced.

"Sod the results," Lisa said viciously, turning sharply with a dancer's grace and pushing through the crowd, out into the hallway.

She bolted down the corridor, her suede soled shoes slipping on the smooth tiles, and took refuge in the toilets, leaning her head against the cool plastic of the cubicle as hot tears trickled down her cheeks.

After a while, she knew she had to go somewhere else. But she couldn't face going back inside yet, and sooner or later someone would come looking for her here. Back out in the corridor, she spotted a fire escape door leading out onto the pavement and took it. Sitting on the steps outside, she rested her head in her hands and listened to the distant sounds of entertainment going on inside. Then a voice came from the next set of doors.

"Lisa?"

She looked up, and there was Red's cousin with her boyfriend Robbie, who she remembered seeing in the photos pinned on the fridge of Rosie's cottage. She hadn't even known they'd come to watch. What must they have thought of her flight? She looked up tearfully, wondering how to explain herself, but Rosie didn't ask, just said, "You must be freezing," and tucked a jacket around her shoulders.

It was made of thick soft fur in three shades of beige. One was so pale it was almost like a stripe of cream, floating on a layer of caramel, which in turn was layered with a rich dark coffee. When she huddled her arms around herself, her fingers sank into the soft pile and she expected to feel the lanolin slipping on her skin as she used to when she pulled sheep's wool off the fences. Of course, there was no lanolin, and no smell of tanned hide. Rosie wouldn't own anything that had once belonged to a dead animal, so the jacket, for all its convincing warmth and texture, smelled only of soap powder.

If she thought hard, Lisa might even know which powder, because it had the same fresh-air field smell as Redmond's T-shirts. The smell brought back the memory of huddling against Redmond a dozen times, at dancing competitions, at home, in his flat, and she wondered whether she believed herself when she said it would never happen again. Was this it? No more gritty salty fingers and greasy chips in the car park, no more rich, flavoursome stews from the Moroccan restaurant, no more gliding around the dance floor as if she was walking on air, her limbs moving in an easy flow with no conscious thought. No more. Could she bear it?

A sob escaped and tears stung Lisa's eyes.

For a few moments she heard nothing over the heaving of her sobs, but then they subsided into slow, dry heaves and she became conscious again of Rosie's presence.

"You must think I'm crazy," Lisa sniffed.

"Not at all. I think it's a very stressful time. And Redmond is a wonderful man but he's not always easy to be with."

"You can say that again," Lisa said, and it all began pouring out. Her doubts, Red's distant manner, the mysterious phone calls… "I don't know what to do," she wailed, and the tears began again.

"Lisa, it's for Redmond to tell you the whole story, but I promise you, it's nothing bad. He just wants to make things work out, and… I don't know… I guess it's the old guy hunter-gatherer thing. He just wants to stalk back into the cave with his haul and impress you, when maybe it would be better if he let you join in. But give him a chance. He's really trying, and I've never seen him care like this before. Whatever dumb things he does, he loves you. I've known him a long time, and I can see it."

Lisa sniffed again and wondered whether she dared let herself believe Rosie.

"Now, come on inside," Rosie continued, "and let's find out what's happened with the competition."

As they walked back into the lobby, Lisa handed back Rosie's jacket.

"Thanks," she said weakly, hoping Rosie knew she didn't just mean for the use of the jacket.

A familiar voice called, "Lisa? Lisa? What's the matter? Are you OK?" Red hurried down the stairs and crossed the lobby to where she and Rosie were standing. Rosie melted away and she was left looking up at Red from tear-filled eyes.

Part of her thought cynically, *The show, that's what it's about. Come over here and stand beside me, so we can face the world as a smiling, lying couple. Then we can win and get your heart's desire: success. But you've been taunting me with the promise of my heart's desire, and I see how much you really love me—when I'm ill and unhappy, all you can say is "the results."*

The angry thoughts brought more hot tears and she pressed her knuckles into her eyes to slow the flood. The pain brought her focus and reluctantly she realised that, no matter how much she wanted to get away from Redmond, she needed to be in the hall for the prize giving for Elaine and Mark's sake. If there was a chance of saving the studio, she couldn't be selfish enough to jeopardise it because of her personal pain. Maybe if they kept it open they'd be able to find a space for her as a full-time teacher, even. That would be a big help with the job situation. And maybe there was a possibility, so slight a possibility that she could hardly even think about it, that she and Redmond would work things out once the pressure of the competition was over.

She straightened up, brushed a hand over the back of her eyes, and looked at her reflection in the glass door. Her eyes were puffy and red, and she'd mussed her hair leaning against the wall. She dabbed a tissue across her eyes, thanking her lucky stars that she was wearing waterproof eyeliner and mascara. Then she gave her hair a cursory smooth and nodded. She was ready to face the world. And Redmond. He was watching her, saying nothing, but with a concerned look in his eyes. Was it real, or manufactured for any watching fans?

She nearly turned and fled again, but his magnetic gaze drew her as much as the gentleness in his voice as he finally asked, "Are you OK? What happened?"

As she hesitated, he took a step towards her and folded her in his arms. She tried not to relax into his embrace.

"I was so worried—I couldn't imagine what would make you miss the results. Are you feeling OK? Do you need a doctor?"

Lisa had almost forgotten her feigned illness. She shook her head mutely.

"Shall we get some air?" Without waiting for an answer, Redmond steered her over to the stairs and sat down, encouraging her to sit down beside him.

"What about the results?" she asked, worried. Now that she'd steeled herself to go back in, she was puzzled to find herself heading in the opposite direction.

"You're more important," he said firmly, keeping his arm over her shoulders to prevent her rising and fleeing.

Lisa blinked at him, bewildered.

"Besides," he continued, "the results will still be the same when we get back."

Lisa shook her head. It might not be true.

"What if they give it to Harry and Tiffany because they're still there?"

"Then they do. There's more to life... I want to know what's happening. What's the matter?" He traced the track of a tear down her cheek with his finger, and the tenderness of the gesture brought a lump to her throat. Was it possible she'd been misled?

She swallowed hard and tried to avoid the subject—it was all too much just now.

"What about Mark and Elaine? We should be there for them." Redmond thumped his fists frustratedly on the shabby stair carpet.

"Let it go, will you? It'll be fine. Look, if you must know, I asked Elaine to ring me when they were actually announcing the results. They're still doing the background stuff at the moment, so you have time to tell me what on earth all this moping is about. Is it about work?"

Lisa shook her head. So… that was why he wasn't worried about the results. His precious mobile meant he wouldn't miss anything important. He could afford to show up here and be all caring and sweet. But the competition was still the most important thing. For a moment there, she'd almost thought otherwise.

"Good," Redmond said briskly. "I don't want you worrying about jobs or money or anything. If you really want to get another job in business, I'm sure you can, but I think you should be dancing anyway, and you won't have trouble getting a job after this. Mark and Elaine would have you like a shot."

"If we don't win, Mark and Elaine won't be able to," Lisa pointed out flatly. It seemed so wrong that the fate of the studio should hang on something as arbitrary as the results of one TV-sponsored competition. She'd battled for weeks to find a way round the situation, but there seemed to be no other way out. If they didn't win, the studio was lost.

"Well…" Redmond said, a little sheepishly.

Lisa looked up sharply. "What?" She knew there was something he hadn't been telling her, but she was baffled as to what it could be, and how it related to the studio.

"You know all the phone calls I've been making?" Redmond sounded embarrassed.

Here it came. He was going to say that they were all to his mystery woman in Florida. Rich and pretty, she would bail the studio out in the blink of an eye if Redmond came back to her. Or something else equally horrible for Lisa to contemplate.

"Well," Redmond said slowly, as if groping for the words to explain. Lisa forgot to breathe as she steeled herself for what was coming next. "You know I have a part share in the studio in Florida?"

Lisa shook her head. She'd assumed he was just employed there.

"Well, I do. I've been putting money in over the years and I've got about a quarter of the studio. Or had, I should say. I've been negotiating to sell my share to one of the other teachers so I don't have to go back. It's been underway for months, but the call this morning was to my lawyers to sort out the last few details."

Lisa stared. It was the last thing she'd imagined.

"When the money comes through, I'll be buying a share in Mark and Elaine's studio. It'll more than cover the renovation work, and hopefully we'll be able to do some more exciting things too, with better premises and more staff. Summer courses. Bigger events—maybe even weddings and things, now that you can have them at civil venues."

"So you're staying here?" Lisa could hear the way her voice suddenly picked up. There seemed to be hope for them after all.

"Would you like me to?" Redmond searched her eyes, and she could see he was waiting eagerly for her answer.

Lisa thought about the nights they'd spent together and how perfectly she fitted into his arms. She thought about how he'd followed her all the way home after the scene in the restaurant, how he'd rescued her, and how he'd been working all this time to push through the sale of the studio so that he could help Mark and Elaine out and stay with her.

And something began to bother her.

"If you've been working on the sale for months," she puzzled, slotting things together in her mind, "you knew we didn't need the competition. So why did you come back for it?"

Redmond laughed.

"Why do you think?"

Lisa shrugged broadly, but her heart leapt. Was he going to say he'd done it for her? What other reason could there be?

"Well, I had to make sure you'd speak to me somehow." He grinned. "I was an idiot, running off the way I did. It was only because I was so scared. I cared about you so much, but I wasn't ready to settle down with you the way everyone would have expected me to. I wanted to make my own way in the world. And I did, but every success got emptier and emptier when you weren't there to share them."

Lisa couldn't remember the last time Redmond had spoken so much. It was that, more than his expression, that made her believe him. Still, the cynical voice in her head put up a last small defence.

"You're sure this isn't just so we can have a big wedding at the studio and get lots of publicity?"

"Lisa," Redmond said exasperatedly, ruffling her hair, "if you want to get married at the top of Snowdon with only the sheep for witnesses, then that's fine with me, so long as you'll marry me."

Lisa smiled with relief and joy. Warmth seemed to flood through her as finally she let herself accept that it was for real. Here she was in the arms of her perfect partner, and that was how she was going to spend the rest of her life. She reached up to seal the unspoken agreement with a kiss, and neither of them moved until the familiar ringing of Redmond's mobile startled Lisa into life.

"Shall we go in?" she asked, and this time she waited for his nod before she set off to face the verdict. Not that it mattered— the studio was safe, and the love in Redmond's eyes as he looked down at her was a better prize than anything the competition had to offer.

It took her most of the way back into the hall to find the words she was looking for. Inside the hall, there was an expectant hush, but Lisa paused outside the door to look up at Redmond and tell him, "You know, whatever happens, I feel like I've won. This competition brought us together, and that's all that matters."

Then she pushed open the door and she and Redmond began the walk back to their seats. This time, looking around, Lisa started to spot faces in the crowd. She could see Rosie and Robbie near the back. And there, further forward, were Mark and Elaine, smiling encouragingly back at her, and next to them, Fritz whispering something in Jerry's ear, which made Lisa smile. Maybe things were finally working out for Jerry.

"And here they are," Phillipa announced, dragging Lisa's mind back to the matter at hand. "Our winners."

Lisa flung herself into Redmond's arms and he held her as if he meant never to let her go.

About the Author

Stephanie Cage lives and writes in the beautiful county of Yorkshire, England. In addition to her day job in administration, she chairs a writing group, is a frequent guest on "Book It" (a literary show on community radio) and tries never to miss an episode of *Strictly Come Dancing*. She has a BA in English Literature from Oxford University and an MA in Creative Writing from Bath Spa, and remembers her student days fondly as much for the ballrooms as the lecture theatres.

In the mood for more Crimson Romance? Check out *All Over the Place* by Serena Clark at *CrimsonRomance.com*.